MY PERFECT RUIN

Perfect Series, Book One

By: Kenadee Bryant

MY PERFECT RUIN

Limitless Publishing, LLC
Kailua, HI 96734
www.limitlesspublishing.com

Formatting: Limitless Publishing

ISBN-13: 978-1-64034-171-5
ISBN-10: 1-64034-171-4

Dedication

To my family,
for always being so supportive of me.

Chapter 1

Layla

"Layla! Come on, you have to come!" my best friend, Kacey Simms, said as we walked down the street toward our apartment.

Kacey was beautiful and if she weren't my best friend, I would be jealous of her. She had long raven-colored hair that framed her face, light blue eyes, and an oval face that made her look like an angel. Kacey was only five-foot-three and one hundred and ten pounds at the most. We've been friends since freshmen year of high school. Back then, she was new, and when I walked into my first class, she immediately came up to me and said, "We will be best friends!" and we've been ever since. We are total opposites, though. Kacey is from a rich family, whereas I come from a poor, dysfunctional one.

Kacey has never rubbed her wealth in my face, however, and neither have her parents. You would think a family with a lot of money would be rude and stuck up, but hers wasn't. They had to be the nicest people I've ever met. They became like my own parents when mine weren't around. If it hadn't been for her and her parents, I wouldn't be where or who I was today.

"Are you even listening to me?" Kacey asked, bringing me out of my thoughts.

"What was that?" I asked.

"I said you need to come to the party tonight."

"Kay, I can't go. You know that," I said, sighing. She's been asking me to go to some classy club with her for weeks now.

"Yes, you can and you will. There are going to be tons of people there, and so many hot guys. Plus, it's a great way to end the weekend!" she said as we came to the doors of our apartment building.

"I don't need to see any hot guys," I protested.

"Oh really? Layla, you have not had a date in over five months and the last one you had sucked. Please, you owe me!"

I groaned, knowing she wasn't going to give up. When she wants something, she is sure to get it. I opened our apartment door and pushed through. Kacey followed behind me, still trying to convince me to go. I loved her to death, but sometimes I really wanted to put a pillow over her head. It was hard to say no to her when she gave me puppy dog eyes or when she pleaded with me nonstop.

"Please, please, please! It's tonight and I know you don't have work tonight," she said, taking off her shoes. I put my phone down and kicked off my own shoes. I tried to block out her talking but knowing she wouldn't stop, I turned to her.

"Fine! I'll go!" I said, not wanting to hear about it anymore.

"Layla, you have…wait, you said yes? Yay," she said, yelling and jumping up and down. "We are going to have a blast! And I already have the perfect outfit picked out for you!"

I just shook my head at her and went to sit on the couch.

Our apartment wasn't huge, but it was pretty good size. Kacey's parents paid for it no matter how many times I told them I would pay half. There were two bedrooms, two bathrooms, a kitchen, and a living room. Both of us had decorated it to make it look homier. If it were possible, I would stay here forever and never leave. I wasn't home very much because I worked long hours, but when I was home I only wore PJs and never left. My job wasn't the best nor the worst. I worked as a waitress in a café on the other side of the bridge. It was an okay job and if I had the opportunity, I would leave.

Our home was New York City. Yes, the busiest city in the world. We both grew up about half an hour away from the city, and when we got accepted into NYU together, we packed up our things and moved to the Big Apple. At first it was hard adjusting to the busy life the city offered, but now, four and a half years later, it was my home. I loved it here and I knew I wouldn't ever leave.

College was fun, but now that I am out, I wish I had chosen a different major. If I had known that places didn't want to hire English majors or that there wouldn't be any jobs involving my degree, I would have chosen something totally different; that, of course, is how I ended up as a waitress. I was suddenly brought out of my thoughts as Kacey walked back into the room carrying a dress in her arms.

"Let's get ready!" she yelled.

"Kacey, we don't have to leave for another hour and a half. And why is it so early?" I said, staring at her from the couch. I was way too comfortable to get up.

"We have to get dressed and do our hair and makeup! We are going earlier 'cause Teddy got us in, and there's cheaper drinks," she said, coming over to me. "Let's go." She grabbed my arm and pulled me up. For a small girl, she was strong. I stumbled against her but before I could right myself, I was pulled toward her bedroom.

"This is your dress," she said, handing me the article of clothing. I looked down at it and saw that it was gorgeous. It was strapless with a long white bottom, and the top was tan with gold all around it. I looked up at Kacey.

"Where did you get this?" I asked, awed.

"Had it in my closet." She shrugged, casual. Don't ask me why she just had a dress like this sitting around her closet. Kacey had a small problem when it came to shopping. If something caught her eye, she would buy it even if she never had a place where she could wear it. Her closet was jam-packed with clothes and she still went out and bought more. Of course, that wasn't a problem when she made pretty good money and her parents were rich.

"I can't wear this." I pushed it back toward

Kacey. No way could I wear something so gorgeous.

"Yes, now put it on," she urged me. I looked toward the bathroom and started toward it.

After taking off my clothes, I slipped into the dress. I left the bathroom to have Kacey help me zip it up. The dress fits like a glove. Turning to the mirror, I gasped at myself. It didn't even look like me. Even though my hair was still in a ponytail, I looked good. The dress made my skin look tanner than it actually was.

"You look great already!" Kacey said from behind me. I smiled at my reflection then looked over at Kacey. I must have been staring at myself longer than I thought because when I turned around, she was already dressed in a tight-fitting red dress that showed all her curves and quite a bit of cleavage. It came to mid-thigh, and she topped it off with a pair of Louboutin high heels.

"Kay, you look sexy," I said, grinning at her. "Are you sure the guys will be all over me?"

"Can't have you hogging them all. Got to do something to make them see me over you."

"Yeah, right."

"Now, we need to get your makeup done."

I made my way over to the chair she had sitting before her mirror, and I sat quietly as Kacey went to work. She always insisted on doing my makeup, which was good since I'm not the best with it. I usually just bypassed it. A few minutes later she was done, but then she went to work doing my hair. I didn't know how long I sat there before she was finally finished with me.

"All done," she said proudly. I smiled and looked in the mirror. My jaw instantly dropped open. She didn't do much, just added a little bit to make it look natural. She had put on bronze eyeshadow to match my dress, and she put enough mascara on to make my gray eyes pop. My brown hair was simply curled and framed my face. Kacey had majored in fashion and was luckily given a job at *Vogue* designing the clothing line. She was amazing and could do whatever she put her mind to.

"I look great, Kay," I said, smiling in thanks. She handed me a pair of nude-colored heels. Luckily, we wore the same size shoe so I could wear hers.

"Wear these." was all she said. They were higher than any other heel I'd ever worn, but I took them.

"You're welcome. Now move your pretty ass. I need to get ready too," she said, shooing me out of the way. Shaking my head at her, I stood up. "Go get your things ready. We need to leave in just a few minutes. And don't you dare ruin your outfit, hair, and makeup or I will kill you," she warned me. I saluted her and left the room.

I got a cute bag out and put in the usual stuff I needed—extra lip gloss, my gum, phone, some money but not too much, ID, and keys to the apartment. Kacey's voice echoed across the hall a few minutes later, telling me it was time to go. Slipping on the heels, I took one last look in the mirror, took a deep breath, and left my room.

***

Ashton

I looked down at my cellphone and saw I had thirty minutes before I had to leave. I went to my closet and picked out something to wear. The only reason I was going to this dumb-ass club was because of my friend Nick. I wasn't in the mood, but I finally gave in and decided to go, but just for a few minutes. I had work to finish before tomorrow.

You could say I am a workaholic, but having to run a million-dollar company makes you that way. If you want to stay at the top, then you have to work hard to stay there.

Tugging on a pair of black dress pants, I grabbed a white button-down dress shirt and rolled up the sleeves. I left a few buttons open and went over to grab my dress shoes. I dried my hair in its usual messy style. Smirking at myself in the mirror, I grabbed my keys and phone then left out the door. Sliding inside the limo, I leaned back and waited to arrive at the club. The only good thing about going to this club was finding a hot girl to take home. My phone started ringing and I answered it.

"What?" I snapped.

"Sir, there has been a situation," one of my advisors said into the phone.

"What situation?" I asked, my eyes narrowing. If he were here, he would be squirming in his seat.

"Some files have gone missing, and we have Watson coming over tomorrow," he said.

"I'm busy. Take care of it, now!" I yelled and hung up. Idiots. Seconds later, the limo came to a stop in front of the club. Clark, my body

7

guard/driver, came around and opened my door. Clark has known me for a long time, and I trusted him. He was my father's bodyguard and driver before me. Nodding in thanks, I slid out of the car. Thankfully there were no cameras here and I could walk inside peacefully. Immediately I was ushered in and shown to the private section where Nick was already seated.

"There you are, man!" he yelled over the music. I simply nodded at him and looked around the room. It was dark and music blared through the speakers, making it almost hard to talk.

"Have a seat, Ash," Nick said, moving to sit on the black couch.

Nick and I have been friends since high school. He's the only one who knows everything about me. After college, I took over the business from my father while Nick invented new technology. We both have become very successful, and I may be a tad more, but we were both two of the most eligible men. We have stuck by each other and even though we get pissed at one another, he is like my brother.

I took a seat on the couch just as a hot waitress came over to me with a glass of scotch. Looking her up and down, I smirked at her and took the scotch. Her breasts seemed to be barely contained inside the material of her shirt, and she wore a very small, tight skirt. The waitress sent me a flirty smile and swayed her hips as she walked away.

"Man, you always have the girls eating out of your hand," Nick said, shaking his head at me while taking a pull of his beer.

"It's my amazing looks and charms," I said,

grinning. We have the reputation of being "womanizers." I use women and I don't care, and they know what they are getting into when they come flirt with me. So, mostly it was their fault, not mine.

"No, I just think they feel sorry for how ugly your face is," he said. I gave him a look, but all he did was chuckle. We sat there staring out over the club and sipping our drinks. I scanned the crowd and came to a stop when I noticed a beautiful brunette stepping through the door.

My eyes narrowed as I stared at her. Her brown hair fell around her shoulders and back in light curls, and her white-and-gold dress swirled around her but also hugged her curves. I knew that, underneath that dress, were legs that went on for miles. She was standing next to a short but pretty dark-haired girl in a tight red dress. I looked her over but instantly went back to the brunette. I watched her as she made her way to the bar with her friend. Something about the way she walked and held herself, I could tell this wasn't her usual scene and that she didn't feel comfortable. I could see her glance around almost nervously, like she felt like she didn't belong.

I sat there staring at her, getting lost in her beauty. All the men around her couldn't take their eyes off of her, me included. As I sat staring at her, the waitress came back with more drinks. She tried getting my attention by sticking her breasts in my face and looking at me suggestively, but I ignored her and stared down at the girl. The waitress finally gave up, and she turned away with a huff.

Something about her drew me in. I stood up and finished my scotch.

"Ashton, where are you going?" Nick asked me.

"I'll be back in a few minutes," was all I said as I left the private area and made my over to the brown-haired cutie.

***

Layla

The moment we stepped into the club, I felt out of place. I followed behind Kacey feeling uncomfortable in my dress, even though compared to half the girls I wasn't showing half as much skin. Even the waitresses wore skimpy clothes. *Ew, glad I don't work here. But then I do have to wear short pants and a tight blouse to work, so maybe it isn't any different.* Kacey walked over to the bar and I trailed behind her. *If I stick by her, I'll be fine,* I told myself.

"Layla, what do you want to drink?" Kacey said into my ear.

"Just a water!" I yelled back over the music.

"No, you're drinking something. Layla, you're twenty-three. Live a little," she yelled. I looked at her, but she kept staring at me. For someone so small and innocent looking, she packed a mean stare. Groaning, I turned to the bartender.

"Do you have any good beer?" I asked loudly. The bartender was a young, cute guy. He looked surprised at my words but went about finding me something.

I wasn't much of a drinker but when I did, I didn't go for fruity drinks. The bartender sat a beer bottle in front of me with a no label. He gave me a wink then went to help his next customers. I took a sip and looked at it approvingly. It was good. As I turned, I ran straight into something hard. I almost stumbled back, but strong arms wrapped around my waist. I looked up and saw a pair of stunning blue eyes staring down at me.

Chapter 2

Layla

I stared up at the striking pair of blue eyes with my jaw hanging wide open. My eyes traveled down the face to see an amazing jaw that was covered with a slight stubble. His face looked like it had been carved by an angel. I couldn't look away. He was the most gorgeous guy I'd ever seen. He had dark brown hair that was almost black, and was styled in a sort of messy but sexy way. As I stood there like a complete idiot staring at him, I saw him smirk, making me realize that I was staring way too long.

"Uh, sorry," I said, trying to back up a little, but the strong arms around me wouldn't let me go far. Kacey stared at us.

"You're good." A deep voice rumbled from above me. My gaze once again snapped to his. "Dance with me," he said, more a demand than a question.

"I—" I started to say, but the man grabbed my

drink from my hand and set it on the bar behind me. He then unwrapped his arms from around my waist to grab my hand. I looked over to my left to have Kacey help me, but all I saw before I was pulled away was her smiling at me and giving me a thumb's up. I was pulled onto the dance floor and into his strong chest. Of course, at that moment a slow song came through the speakers. *Great,* I thought sarcastically. I stood there awkwardly for a few seconds as we swayed back and forth before I found my voice.

"I...uh...what's your name?" I asked, looking up at him. Even when I was in five-inch heels, he was still way taller than me. He looked strangely familiar as well.

"Ashton. And yours?" he asked, tightening his hold on me, bringing me somehow closer to him.

"Layla."

"A pretty name for a pretty girl," Ashton said, trying to use a pick up-line on me. I couldn't help myself as I burst out laughing.

"Does that line ever work?" I asked, laughing still. The look on his face was of shock and amusement, like he didn't expect me to catch him on it.

"On most women, yes," he said, his expression turning to amusement.

"I'm not like most women," I replied. I heard him mutter something but couldn't quite hear it.

A part of me was yelling at myself, asking me why I was flirting with someone I literally just ran into. As I stood there staring up at him, I realized how wide and hard his shoulders were underneath my fingers. Swaying back and forth to the beat of the music, I looked him over. He was intimidating; he seemed to exude an aura of wealth and power. I could see why everyone moved out of his way when he walked by, or stared at him in awe. I couldn't help but feel intimidated. You definitely didn't want to cross him in a dark alley.

"You look beautiful in that dress," he said, looking me up and down. A blush crept onto my face, and I looked at his chest, which was in front of me.

"What are you doing here?" I asked once I got my voice back. I felt him shrug under my hands.

"Looking for you," he said, wiggling his eyebrows sexily at the cheesy line. I couldn't help but roll my eyes.

"You need to work on your pickup lines. They are terrible," I said truthfully. I bet he got plenty of women; I just hoped he would say something better next time.

"You think so? I think they are great."

"Yeah, keep up with them and I bet you will have women falling in no time," I said, grinning at him.

"Who says I don't?"

"Cocky," I said, not paying attention. Then I realized that the song had changed and that people were staring at us.

"Hmm," Ashton said, smirking slightly. The corner of his mouth tilted up slightly. Yep, that was me noticing things about a complete stranger. For some reason, I could tell he smirked more than he smiled, but I bet when he smiled it made him look hotter.

"What are you doing here?" he asked, breaking me out of my trance.

"Oh, you know, looking for hot guys to get my claws on," I said, keeping my face straight. He raised an eyebrow at me.

"Hot guys?"

"Yep," I said then looked around the dance floor. "See that guy over there with the big glasses and going bald? That is sexy," I said, gesturing with my head over to the guy across the dance floor. I looked up to see Ashton's expression and almost burst out laughing. He had his eyes narrowed at the poor guy and I saw his jaw was clenched. I would have not said anything, but I felt bad for the poor guy.

"Stop. The poor guy is going to shit is pants," I said, slapping the back of Ashton's head. He turned his gaze to me and I almost flinched back from his glare. "I was kidding."

"Did you just hit me?" he asked, his eyes wide now. It was almost like he'd never gotten hit by a woman before.

"Yes, you deserved it," I said simply. Silence made its way around us as we swayed side to side, even though the song was fast and upbeat. The song once again changed, but this time I realized I should be going. I kept trying to pull away but I couldn't seem to. His hard body felt good against mine. I even enjoyed his breath on top of hair and neck. Finally, with a lot of coaxing from my brain, I pulled away from Ashton's warm body.

"Well, thank you for the dance, or dances," I said, moving out of his arms.

"You're leaving?" he asked, reaching for my waist again but I took another step back.

"Yeah. I have to get going."

"It's only eight." *Wow, we've been here for three hours already?* I thought.

"I have plans," I said, even though all I planned to do was order pizza, change into my PJs, and watch TV. He stared down hard at me. For a second I was tempted to stay…okay, maybe I was more than tempted to stay but I knew I shouldn't. "It was great meeting you. Get some better pickup lines." I smiled and turned to walk away. "Bye." I knew that if I stayed any longer, I would do something I'd regret.

I made my way over to Kacey and saw she was with a tall, good-looking guy. Smiling apologetically, I butted in.

"Sorry for interrupting, but can I borrow you for a second?" I said to Kacey. She nodded and I pulled to a few feet away. "I'm going to go home."

"What? Why? I thought you were dancing with that sexy guy you almost spilt your drink on?" she asked, slightly angry.

"It was good, but I'm getting a headache. You stay, though," I said.

"No, I'll come home with you."

"No. Stay. You seemed to be having a good conversation with that guy. I'll get a cab and I'll meet you at home." I knew she didn't want to leave and I was fine with that.

"But—" she started to say.

"No buts. I'll be fine. Stay and have fun. Just don't drink too much and be home at a reasonable time."

"Okay, Mom," she said sarcastically. "Thank you! I'll be home soon, I promise," she added.

"Bye." I hugged her and made my way to the door.

Stepping out of the bar, I took a deep breath. With the sun down, it was slightly chilly but not cold. Thankfully, one of the bouncers outside hailed me a cab. I was instantly glad Kacey and I came earlier, because a long line went all away around the block. Smiling in thanks to the bouncer, I got inside the cab and give him my address. As the car started forward, I stared out the window. Ashton's face popped inside my head and I couldn't help but smile. Something about him seemed very familiar, but I couldn't quite put my finger on it. For someone I just met, he plagued my thoughts the minute I walked away from him. The car stopped, so I paid the driver and got out. Not paying attention, I didn't realize I was not in front of my apartment building until the taxi was gone.

I was standing in front of a black, empty street. I glanced around starting to get scared. I didn't know what was down the dark street, and I didn't really want to find out. Knowing I couldn't just stand there, I walked back toward the direction I came, hopefully toward the club. The only sound that could be heard was the click of my heels. I tried to take my thoughts away from the bad things that could happen to me. I was so busy talking to myself that I didn't hear voices and footsteps until it was too late. I whipped around and came face-to-face with five very large, mean-looking guys. I unconsciously took a step back but they did the same, following me.

"Look what we have here. Are you lost?" one of the guys said, coming forward. I couldn't answer. My voice was caught in my throat. I could tell my eyes were wide and scared. I should have just stayed at the club or even paid more attention when the taxi driver stopped. I'd always heard the stories about walking alone at night in New York City, but I never really paid any mind to them until now.

The group of guys got closer and I started freaking out. *I'm too young to die!* I screamed inside. I would have laughed at how dramatic that sounded, but with the situation at hand, I couldn't really laugh. Normally someone would be praying, thinking about their family members and what dying would do to them, or even saying their last goodbyes, but not me. I stood there thinking about how my parents wouldn't even care if I died right now in a ditch. They'd probably throw a party, actually. The thought of my parents made me sad, but for some reason, I couldn't see why. They never loved me. Hell, they never liked me honestly. But it's weird that is what my mind immediately went to. Not even the thought of screaming entered my mind. The sound of the men's voices right in front of me tugged me out of my thoughts.

I looked at the guy in the lead, not sure what he was saying. My body was numb from fear and the realization that something was going to happen to me. I heard the slap before I felt it. My head snapped to the side, and I staggered back a step. My hand flew up to my cheek. Before the guy could take another hit or move closer, the sound of screeching tires echoed around us. All heads snapped up as bright lights blinded us. I squinted and stood still, not knowing if the person inside the car were here to help or not.

All five men stood watching the car, glaring. Time seemed to stand still as the car door opened and a tall silhouette stepped out. My breath hitched in my throat as I heard a familiar voice say something…Ashton? With the car only a few feet in front of me, I did the first thing that I could think of: I ran toward Ashton's car. I flew past a surprised-looking Ashton standing in front of the open door and jumped inside. He must have realized what I was doing, because he quickly slid in after me, telling the driver to drive. The car was peeling away before Ashton even shut the door. I glanced through the back window and saw the group of men starting for the car, but they stopped once they obviously realized it was no use. I let out a loud sigh and slumped against the comfortable leather of the seat.

About five minutes later, the car came to a stop in a parking garage. I didn't know where we were, but I wasn't too frightened. Ashton opened the door and stepped out, waiting for me to follow. I stumbled out of the car and to his side. The limo pulled away and his hand on my lower back guided me to the elevators straight across from us.

The ride up the elevator was silent and awkward. My cheek throbbed and my body felt exhausted. I was ready to crawl into bed and forget this whole thing ever happened. Thankfully, the elevator came to a stop a minute later, and I followed Ashton out and down a hallway. We stopped in front of a door, and he entered a code before throwing the door open. When he gestured for me to go in, I squeezed past him and entered what I could only guess was his apartment. When I walked in, I froze.

My mouth dropped open when I caught sight of the room. It was huge like a penthouse! Everywhere I looked I couldn't help but gawk at everything. *How can he afford this?* I thought to myself as Ashton took me into a bathroom.

"Where are we?" I finally asked as I watched Ashton move around the bathroom looking for something. I stood awkwardly off to the side.

"My apartment. Hop up on the counter." I wanted to ask why but instead, I did what he asked.

"Apartment? More like a penthouse," I said, amazed at the size of the bathroom. It seemed to be a spare one, but it had a long granite counter with two sinks, a toilet, and dark wood cabinets. Everything about the bathroom screamed money to me. All Ashton did was shrug. He moved around the room quickly and then came and stood in front of me. Gently he pushed my knees apart and stood in-between them. I stared up at him trying to not show how I was affected by his touch.

"This may burn," Ashton said, bringing a cotton ball to my cheek. "You have a slight cut on your bottom lip," he added, probably in response to my confused look. I nodded and held still. I felt a stab of pain the instant he touched my cheek. I gripped the counter and bit my bottom lip so I wouldn't make a sound, but pain laced across my bottom lip. I let go of my lip and hissed. The pain went away a minute later. Honestly, the pain was not the worse I'd ever felt; it was actually a speck compared to other times I'd been hurt. Ashton started wiping my cheek and bottom lip softly while looking to see where else I was hurt.

"Ashton, stop, I'm fine," I said as he kept wiping my face. He reluctantly stopped and threw the cotton ball in the toilet.

"Does your cheek hurt?" Ashton asked, looking down at me.

"No, it's fine," I said, shaking my head and looking into his blue eyes.

"It's bruised and swollen."

"Nothing I can't take," I replied honestly. Punches, even a few kicks were nothing to a smack on the cheek. "Thank you, by the way."

I looked up and saw his blue eyes staring down at me. Something about the way he looked at me made my heart flutter. I sat there on the counter staring up at Ashton, my stomach doing flips. I didn't know how he found me in the alley, but I was thankful and I couldn't think of how I would ever repay him. I watched as he slowly came closer to me. My eyes latched onto his lips and I couldn't look away. My body instantly started to move toward him and in a split second, my mouth was against his.

Chapter 3

Layla

My fingers made their way up and through Ashton's hair. It was thick and soft, just how it looked. Even though his lips were soft, they were hard and demanding. Instinctively, my lips moved against his just as hard, and my legs started to wrap around his waist. A small moan started in my throat and threatened to break free. Just as quick as the kiss started, it ended. Before I could even open my eyes, I felt Ashton untangle my legs from his waist and take a step back. The warmth of his body left me and I sat there stunned and cold. *What—*

"There's a spare toothbrush in the far drawer to your left. I'll go get you some clothes," Ashton said coldly and turned and left the bathroom. I stared after him, confused. *Did I do something wrong?* He basically just kissed me, then suddenly pulled away, told me my breath stank, and left. *Great.*

I slid off the counter and carefully landed on my feet. I put a hand to my tingling lips. *Wow, that was a great kiss.*

Deciding it was easier to stand and walk, I slipped off my heels and placed them on the counter. I took a deep breath to get myself ready to look in the mirror, and I was glad I did. My hair looked like a bird had made a nest in it, my makeup was smeared, and my cheek and lip were swollen and taking on a purple color already. I groaned. No wonder Ashton made a quick getaway. *Wonder what Kacey's going to say about my face tomorrow,* I pondered. She didn't know a lot about what my parents did to me. The only reason she found out was when I was put in the hospital one day. I had made her promise to not say anything to anyone, especially her parents.

As high school went on and my beatings got worse, it was becoming harder to conceal my bruises. On most days, I would leave for school extra early and head to Kacey's house so she could help me cover the bruises on my face and neck. I always joked I helped Kacey learn how to do makeup better, but she never found it funny. Sighing at my thoughts, I shook my head.

Taking Ashton's advice, I made my way toward the drawer where the spare toothbrushes would be. Brushing my teeth, I stared at my reflection. I stared at the bruise. I couldn't help but think of my family. It'd been about three or four years since I'd been hit. The beatings used to be so regular that I had gotten used to it, but now, after years of peace, my cheek stung and throbbed. I was so focused on my past I didn't hear Ashton knocking and calling my name. When the door opened and Ashton started shaking my shoulder, I finally came out of it.

"Huh?" I asked.

"I just said I found you some clothes. I only have men's clothes so I hope they fit," he said plainly, handing me what he had.

"Thank you," I said, taking the clothes. All he did was nod and leave the room, closing the door behind him again. I looked down at the clothes and saw he brought me a gray t-shirt and a pair of boxers. Smiling, I set them on the counter next to my heels and reached back to undo my dress. My hands fumbled with the zipper. After a few minutes of struggling, I gave up. *Damn it.* Sighing, I opened the door and peeked around for Ashton. Seeing no one, I called out for him.

"Ashton?" I called. I waited but didn't see him. "Ashton?" I called out louder. A second later, he came into view from down the hall.

"Yes?" he asked.

"I, uh." I blushed and bit my bottom lip. "I can't unzip my dress," I said. All he did was smirk and gesture for me to turn around. Looking down at the ground, I turned. I felt a warm hand press against my shoulder blades while the other went to my zipper. I felt him start to unzip my dress and I grabbed the front so I wouldn't flash him. The lower the zipper went, the lower Ashton's hand followed. I suppressed a shiver that wanted to make its way down my spine. Embarrassed by my reaction, I whispered a soft "Thank you" and disappeared in the bathroom.

I leaned against the door and breathed deeply. I wanted to yell at my stupid body for reacting like that to someone I just literally barely met. After a good few minutes of yelling at myself, I went to get dressed. Peeling the dress off of me, I slipped into the gray shirt and boxers. The shirt was really big but smelled half cologne and half pure male. Don't think I'm a weirdo because trust me, the smell could make any girl fall to her knees. The boxers were like shorts to me, and were surprisingly nice and soft.

Looking around the bathroom, I finally found a brush and I almost jumped in joy. No way was I going back out there looking like a mess. Brushing my hair took a while, but thankfully I got it tangle free, the waves from earlier almost flat. Taking one last look in the mirror, I left the bathroom with my dress and heels in my hand. I was blindly walking through Ashton's "apartment." I turned in the direction I'd seen Ashton walk down to see if I could find him. I came to an abrupt stop and my jaw fell open. The hall had made a left turn and opened to the living room I was in before, where there was a doorway that looked like it led to the kitchen, and a staircase leading to who knows where. *Wow, this place is amazing!* I thought.

In the living room sat a big and comfy-looking black leather couch, a huge seventy-two-inch TV, and end tables with cool lamps. The walls were painted a pretty deep blue that made the room seem even more cozy and casual. I didn't really expect to see a guy's place look this good. Setting my dress and shoes on the couch, I padded barefoot over to the doorway leading to a kitchen. I let out a soft whistle. The place was huge! The counter was pure granite, a color mixed with light and dark. Dark wood cabinets lined the kitchen walls, looking great with the dark red wall. I ran my fingers across the flat-top stove, as well as the sink and counter tops.

The kitchen was my dream kitchen. I knew inside the cabinets were every pot you could think of, and maybe more. I loved to cook even though I only had a little bit of money and it wasn't that fancy. Don't get me wrong, ramen can be very classy, but only the first time. After that, it becomes boring. *Man, this guy has everything*, I thought to myself. I opened the stainless-steel fridge and looked inside. It was packed with stuff. I grabbed a bottle of water, hoping it was okay. Glancing around, I decided I better go find Ashton and figure out how I was getting home.

Starting up the stairs, I ran through several responses in my head on how to thank Ashton for saving me. I didn't even want to think what would have happened if he hadn't shown up. I didn't know what they would have done to me, but I was just thankful that everything was okay now. Once I reached the top of the steps, I took a deep breath and went forward.

"Uh, Ashton?" I called out.

"In here!" he called from down the hall. I followed the voice and came to a bedroom that looked even bigger than the living room downstairs. *How much money does this guy have?* I wondered. I walked through the door and saw Ashton standing at the foot of the bed unbuttoning his shirt. "There you are." He turned toward me and I saw his shirt was half unbuttoned. My mouth went dry, and I unconsciously moved toward the bed. It was not like me to stare openly at someone, but I couldn't tear my eyes away from Ashton's body.

Taking a seat on the edge of the huge bed, I stared at him. I watched as his long fingers swiftly unbuttoned the last of his buttons. To say he was fit was an understatement. His chest was nice and hard, and he had an eight-pack that was so defined that a diamond could probably break if it hit it. The suit he wore did him no justice; he was twice as good-looking without it. I knew I was staring, but I couldn't pull my eyes away. This was literally something out of a movie. Someone like me has never and probably will never see this ever again, so I was going to look away all I want.

"Like what you see?" His voice jerked me away from staring at his washboard abs up to his blue eyes. He stared down at me in amusement.

"I, uh." I tried to say something, but my tongue got twisted.

"Thought so." He raised an eyebrow at me then went to take off his pants.

"What are you doing?" I yelled, covering my eyes even though every fiber of my body wanted to look.

"Getting undressed. It's not my fault you walked in on me undressing." He continued pulling his slacks off. He threw them at me and they landed on my head. I uncovered my eyes and glared at him. He stood in front of me in just his boxers. I tried to hide my expression, even though my body was going into overdrive. *Stupid hormones!* I shouted at myself.

"These belong to you," I said, grabbing his pants and throwing them back at him. He smirked at me and caught them one-handed.

"Don't act like you don't want some of this." He gestured to his almost-naked body. I just rolled my eyes and got more comfortable on the bed. As I stared at his body, my mouth went dry. I was sitting there waiting for myself to wake up and realize this was all a dream. With his back turned to me, I pinched my arm and bit back a yelp. Yup, this was real and I wasn't dreaming.

"Whatever you say," I said, acting like none of this was affecting me. He just gave me a look and went to his walk-in closet. With him out of view, I slumped my shoulders. I couldn't even form thoughts as to what I was doing or did for that matter. Layla Kingston would never had gone home with a stranger, let alone kissed him. *Layla, just stay calm. You're okay. Everything will be fine. Everything will go back to normal tomorrow. He will just drop you off at home then go on with his life, and you can as well.* Calming down slightly, I closed my eyes and tried to stifle a yawn.

When I glanced over at the alarm clock on his bedside table, my eyes widened. It was almost one in the morning. *How long was I down that alley? How long was I in the bathroom?* No wonder I was tired. I'd been up for twenty hours. Getting up at a quarter to five was now kicking me in the ass. Exhaustion came in waves all of a sudden. Another yawn escaped my lips just as Ashton walked back in. He was still shirtless but was now in a pair of basketball shorts, and his hair looked brushed.

"Can you take me home?" I asked quietly once I had found my voice. I was still having such a hard time forming sentences.

"At one in the morning? I don't think so. You'll stay here," he said, coming toward me. My eyelids became heavy as he grabbed my hand, pulling me up. Ashton stopped me from saying otherwise by shushing me and practically pushing me onto the bed. I didn't have the energy to protest, so I slid beneath the covers. All of the events from tonight were catching up to me, and my body yearned for sleep.

Ashton slid in beside me and pulled the covers up over us. I mumbled a thank you and sunk down into the soft, comfortable mattress, forgetting about the men in the alley, kissing a complete stranger, and now sleeping in his bed. Everything slipped my mind as sleep pulled me into its grasp. The last thing I felt was a pair of strong arms wrap around my stomach, turn me on my side, and pull me back against something hard and warm. I sighed and sunk into a deep slumber.

Chapter 4

Layla

I woke up with my face pressed against something hard and warm. Warm breath blew against the back of my neck, making me shiver slightly. I slowly cracked open my eyes and lifted my head slightly. Looking down, I saw a bare chest. I turned my head and saw Ashton dead asleep, with me on top of him. *How did I end up like this?* I asked myself.

As I stared at him, I couldn't help but think about how cute he looked when he slept. Even though his hair was sticking up and his mouth was wide open, he still looked hot, if that were even possible. His heavy arm was draped against my waist, keeping me against him. I wanted to run my fingers through his hair, but I resisted the urge in case he woke up. I had the feeling that when he woke up and saw me staring at him and draped against him, he wouldn't be that happy.

I tried smiling softly at him, but my cheek pulled

painfully and I grimaced in pain. I prayed that he wouldn't wake up as I slowly moved out from under his arm. The gods must have been listening or something because I was able to get out from under his heavy arm and out of the comfortable bed. I glanced at the time and saw it was eight. *Crap, I have to be at work in two hours*, I thought bitterly. It wasn't like I hated my job…okay, I hated it a lot but it was the only place that paid me a fair amount of money so I could pay my bills. Staring down at Ashton one last time, I smiled sadly then turned to leave.

As silently as I could, I made my way down the stairs to the living room. Grabbing my dress and heels, I went in search for the bathroom I used before. Once I found it, I quickly changed but kept the heels off. Holding them and the clothes Ashton let me wear, I made my way toward the front door. I took once last look around the apartment. I opened the front door and quietly shut it behind me. I walked over to the elevator and got in. The entire way down, I couldn't help but think about what has happened in the last twenty-four hours.

The elevator came to a stop and opened up. I took a deep breath and stepped out. Before the doors closed, I took one last look at Ashton's door. It almost seemed like once the doors closed, everything that happened would go away, like dust in the wind. Once the elevator door closed, Ashton would fade into a memory, like I would for him. Reluctantly, the doors closed and I stood there staring like an idiot. It was weird how I felt like I was missing something when I got off the elevator.

Just a moment with Ashton and I felt connected to him, as weird as that probably sounded.

Turning around, I made my way out the building. I passed by people, and everyone looked at me, some even stopping to stare. I couldn't imagine what they were seeing. I bet my hair was everywhere from sleeping, my cheek black and purple, and plus I was wearing at party dress at eight in the morning. Ignoring the stares, I made it to the door and thankfully the doorman opened it for me.

"Miss, do you need me to call you a cab?" he asked me.

"That would be nice. Thank you." I smiled thankfully. He nodded at me then followed behind me. He stood on the curb and waved down a taxi.

"Here you go, miss." He opened the door for me.

"Thank you so much." Smiling at the doorman in thanks, I slid inside the cab and told driver my address.

The whole way there I made sure that the driver was really taking me home, not like last night. As I sat there lost in my thoughts, I only vaguely realized that I left my phone at Ashton's place. Once the taxi pulled to my apartment, I got out, glad that I made sure to put my money back in the top of my dress. Paying the man, I opened the front door and made my way up the stairs. When I opened the door to mine and Kacey's, I was instantly bombarded with a yell and something hard hitting me, making me fall against the closed door.

"Where the hell have you been?" someone yelled in front of me. Peeking from under my bangs, I saw

Kacey standing in front of me with her hands on her hips and a look that could kill.

"I—" I started but she interrupted me.

"You've had me worried sick. I thought you were murdered or kidnapped or something! What happened to 'I'm just going home. I'll see you at home.'"

"Sorry, I—"

"And here you are in last night's clothes at eight in the morning, been god knows where, doing god knows what, while I was here worrying sick about you. And you didn't even think to call me! Your best friend!"

"Kacey—" She kept yelling at me. Every time I tried to say something, she would keep talking. By now she was pacing back and forth, stopping every so often to point at me.

"Layla, I…what the *hell* happened to your face?" When she saw my face, she froze for a second before charging toward me and gripping my chin.

"Ow, Kacey, stop!" I finally yelled and ripped away from her. Somehow, I was able to squeeze by her and fell onto the couch. "First, I'm sorry I kept you up worrying over me. I didn't mean for that to happen. After I left the club, things became…a tad crazy, and some things happened and I'm sorry. As for my face and why I'm late, I'll explain after I go shower and take these clothes off, okay? After that, then I'll tell you everything you want to know," I said, taking a deep breath and getting up once again.

Not giving Kacey a chance to answer, I pushed past her and into my bedroom. Thankfully, she followed me and helped me out of the dress without saying a word. She seemed to get I needed a few minutes to get cleaned up. Smiling at her, I went into the bathroom to shower. I was lucky to have Kacey as my best friend. She knew when to say something and when not to. Plus, she knew when I needed a shoulder to cry on or someone to give me advice. I made sure that when I get out of the shower I'll hug her and tell her everything that has happened.

***

Ashton

Stop kissing her, goddammit! Stop! Stop!

I pulled my lips away from her soft ones and unwrapped her legs around my waist. I didn't want to stop kissing her, but the rational voice inside my head was screaming at me to stop, and that it wasn't right. For some reason, I didn't want to hurt her and lead her on. Ignoring the sad look on her face when I pulled away, I stiffened my expression and spoke.

"There are spare toothbrushes in the drawer over there. I'll go get you some clothes," I said, sounding cold. I didn't spare a glance back at her and left the bathroom. Standing outside the door for a minute to get myself under control, I headed toward my room to get some clothes for Layla. As much as I wanted to see her in lingerie left behind by other women, I chose a pair of my boxers and a plain gray t-shirt for her instead.

Heading back downstairs to the bathroom, I knocked and waited for her to answer. A minute went by and still no answer. I knocked again, pretty loudly. Getting fed up and slightly worried, though I wouldn't admit it, I reached for the door handle and felt it was unlocked. Opening it, I walked in and saw Layla standing there brushing her teeth and staring into the mirror with a glazed-over expression. It seemed like she wasn't here and was off somewhere else, or lost in thought. Getting more worried, I shook her shoulder and she finally snapped out of her thoughts.

She turned toward me and looked at me in surprise. A small part of me couldn't stop myself from admiring how beautiful her gray eyes were.

"Huh?" she asked.

"I just said that I brought you some clothes. I only have men's, so I hope they fit," I replied. Suppressing my feelings, I made sure my face was void of emotion. I was used to doing it, as sad as that may be. Nodding once at her, I turned and left again. I knew I was being rude, but I didn't want this to turn into anything. *I'm just here helping her out, then taking her home tomorrow,* I told myself. Before I made it to the stairs to go and change, I heard Layla calling my name. *What*—I turned back. Coming around the corner, I saw her standing in the middle of the hallway looking lost.

"Yes?" I asked.

"I, uh." She blushed and bit her bottom lip. I sighed inwardly. "I can't unzip my dress," she said quietly. Smirking, I gestured for her to turn around. Putting my hand in between her shoulder blades, I started unzipping her dress. I noticed a shiver went down her spine as my hands trailed lower, following the zipper. Just as I got to the end of the zipper, Layla mumbled a quiet "Thank you" and ran off to the bathroom, shutting the door.

Shaking my head at myself, I made my way through my apartment and to my room. The apartment was clean as always and everything was in order. In a way, I had OCD because I didn't like anything out of place. Once in my room, I threw my phone, wallet, and keys on my bedside table before unbuttoning my dress shirt sleeves.

Seeing Layla's cheek all swollen and already purple, I couldn't help but feel bad. *If only I had gotten there sooner,* I thought. A little voice inside my head made me stop for a second. *Why is it your responsibility to make sure she's okay? Why do you even care about what has happened to her? Ashton, you literally just met her seven hours ago. You don't know her and should not give a shit about her.* When I heard Layla's soft voice call out my name, I yelled, "Here."

I turned around and saw Layla walking into the room and my heart almost stopped. Even wearing my boxers and oversized t-shirt, she still looked sexy. She somehow made it look sexy when others would just look stupid or like a drowning rat. Biting the inside of my cheek, I stared at her. As she took a seat on my bed, her long tan legs came into view and I had to stop myself from going over there and jumping on top of her. I started unbuttoning my dress shirt, and shrugged it off.

"Like what you see?" I asked, staring at her in amusement. Her eyes raked up and down my body. To say I was fit was right. I made sure I worked out a good two hours every day and ate healthy. My body was hard, and it definitely helped with the ladies. A combination of being a billionaire, a bachelor, and having a nice body are exactly what girls want.

"I, uh."

"Thought so," I said, raising an eyebrow as I reached for my pants.

"What are you doing?" she yelled, covering her eyes like a five-year-old.

"Getting undressed. It's not my fault you walked in on me undressing." Pulling off my pants I threw that at her, hitting her on the head. She glared at me, but it didn't move me at all.

"These belong to you," Layla said and threw them back at me. Smirking at her, I caught them.

"Don't act like you don't want some of this." I gestured to my practically naked body and made my way to my closet.

"Whatever you say." She was trying to act like I didn't affect her, but I could tell by her voice that she was affected somehow, even if she's trying to hide it.

I went into my closet. I usually didn't wear pajamas, but I didn't want the last string of my self-restraint to snap. Taking a deep breath after changing, I came out and saw Layla sitting there looking tired. I could see she was trying to fight it, but wasn't succeeding. Smirking, I made my way toward her.

"Can you take me home?" Layla asked quietly, her eyelids obviously getting heavier and heavier.

"At one in the morning? I don't think so. You'll

stay here," I said, grabbing her hand and pulling her up. Pulling her to the top of the bed, I softly pushed her down. Going around to the other side, I slid into bed as well and pulled the covers up over us. She mumbled something, but I couldn't make out what it was. Smiling, I turned her around and wrapped my arms around her pulling her tight against me. Unconsciously she snuggled deeper into my body, and we both drifted off to sleep.

***

I woke up the next morning to an empty bed. Groaning as I sat up, I rubbed my eyes and looked around. This was the first time a girl left *me* alone in bed. It was usually me who left or kicked *them* out. Shaking my head at how different that girl was, I got up out of bed and stretched my muscles. Even though today was a Saturday, I had a meeting at one, as well as some work to finish up. Glancing at the clock, I saw it was 8:30. I had about five hours before I had to be at the restaurant. I decided on working out, but made my way to the kitchen first to grab a cup of coffee.

When I pressed the brew button, the coffee pot came to life grinding up the coffee beans. Opening a cabinet, I grabbed a mug and set it on the counter. Even though I had only gotten a few hours of sleep these last couple of days, I had to force myself not to crawl back in bed. A minute later, the coffee stopped and I poured myself a mug. Taking my coffee black, I grabbed it and leaned against the counter sipping it. My thoughts drifted to Layla once again, and for some unknown reason I kept seeing her face in front of me and feeling her body pressed against mine.

Something about her drew me in. Honestly, she wasn't even my type. I liked a girl who was tall, long legged, big breasted, had a nice ass, and looked like a model. Layla wasn't any of those things, but she was still pretty somehow. Shaking my head at even thinking about her anymore, I drained my cup and made my way to my gym room. The apartment had four bedrooms and I only occupied two; my bedroom and office I used when I worked at home. With two spare rooms, I turned one into a gym and another where Nick could crash when he stayed over, which was somewhat often, and where I slept with girls. I didn't let them in my bedroom. Glad I was already wearing basketball shorts and no shirt, I went straight over to the treadmill to run.

***

Layla

I sat there quiet after I had just finished telling Kacey everything. Kacey had been sitting there with her mouth wide open for the last five minutes, and I was getting worried her mouth would be getting dry, or a bug might fly in there. Leaning back on my bed, I ran my fingers through my freshly washed hair. I had just finished showering as Kacey burst into my room and demanded I tell her everything or she wouldn't move from my bed.

"Kacey?" I asked her, deciding it was time to see

if she were still alive. Waving my hand in front of her did nothing. Getting kind of fed up, I pinched one of her cheeks hard and was rewarded with a yell and a slap to the hand. Smiling, I looked at her. "Better?"

"I just…wow" was all she said.

"I know." I leaned back again against my pillows and sighed. Everything that had happened seemed so unreal. Never in a million years would I have danced with someone as handsome as him, nor gone home with him. *Well, technically nothing even happened.* I knew that was true, but a small part of me wanted to live up the fact that I, Layla Kingston, stayed at a very hot man's house. The only downfall was I knew he would or already had forgotten about me, and I didn't even know who he was.

"What was his name again?" Kacey asked suddenly, knocking me out of my thoughts.

"Um, Ashton something. He never told me his last name," I said with sudden realization. *Nice, Layla. If you wanted him to find you, he doesn't even know your full name!*

"That name sounds very familiar," she said with her brow furrowed.

"Yeah, because thousands of guys have that name," I pointed out.

"No, that's not why. Wait a minute!" Getting up, she left my room. I was confused. A second later, she came bounding into my room again with her laptop. She plopped onto my bed and opened the screen and turned it on.

"Care to tell me why you grabbed your laptop and are practically bouncing up and down?" I asked, watching as her laptop loaded.

"Because that name's so familiar and I have to search it up."

"How? Facebook?" I scoffed.

"Yes, and Google," Kacey said in a "duh" tone as she clicked on the Safari icon. I stayed silent as she did her thing. She went onto Google and typed in the name "Ashton" and pressed enter. I couldn't even count how many results popped up.

"How about images? If you see him, then we can find out what his full name is and see what he does and stuff."

"Okay," I agreed as she clicked images.

Instantly, pictures of all different kinds of guys popped up. Just as I was looking at the first line of pictures, one stuck out at me. I gasped when I saw it was Ashton. Kacey must have seen my face and followed my eyes to the picture. I couldn't talk, and she clicked on his picture. A site pulled up, and I couldn't help but gasp. The site that popped up showed a big photo of Ashton and had an article underneath it. As I started reading it, my eyes got larger and larger the more I read.

Ashton was *the* Ashton Miller! Multimillionaire, playboy, and sexiest bachelor in New York City!

Chapter 5

Layla

Ashton freaking Miller! I had danced, gone home, kissed, and slept in the same bed as the most famous bachelor and richest man in New York. Never mind that he saved me from being hurt. I sat there staring at the computer screen, still in shock.

"Damn, girl! You slept with a millionaire!" Kacey shouted.

"Kacey! It wasn't even that kind of slept. It was actual sleep," I said, making sure she got that I didn't have sex with Ashton.

"Whatever! You still slept with him," she said, looking at me. "You actually did something interesting!"

"What do you mean I actually did something interesting?" I asked, insulted.

"Come on, Lay! You know it's true. You haven't done anything interesting since…never! Not even in college. This could be something that could turn into something great."

"Kay, that could never happen. He has already forgotten about me by now. Plus, I don't even know him at all. Hell, I didn't even know he was a millionaire."

"Lay—"

"Kacey, come on. I need to get ready for work," I said, getting up and heading to my closet to get out my work uniform.

"Layla, you won't know unless you try," was all she said as she stood up, wrapped an arm around me, then left my room. I stood there for a minute thinking about what she said. She might be right, but I wouldn't be "trying" anything out. It usually didn't work out anyways. Sighing, I changed into my work uniform and went to put my hair up into a ponytail. Looking at the clock, I saw that it was ten. I had twenty minutes to get to work. My work uniform consisted of a black skirt—a short one I might add—and a tight black shirt that showed a tad bit too much cleavage for my liking. Somehow the uniform passed as presentable for such a highly rated restaurant. Slipping on my high heels—also part of the uniform—I started on my makeup. I didn't put on much, just a light layer of foundation, a swipe of my mascara, and a little eyeshadow. I couldn't just show up to work looking terrible because this was my only job, and neither could I complain about the uniform.

Walking out of my room, I quickly looked around for my phone. Looking on the couch, the counter, and even under pillows, I couldn't find it.

"Kay, have you seen my phone?" I called out to her.

"I haven't!" she yelled from her room. Sighing, I gave up looking knowing I wouldn't have time to search anymore. I grabbed my jacket, as it was starting to get cold with winter coming, and my purse.

"I gotta go, Kacey. I'll see you around five or so!" I yelled as I made my way out the door. I heard her yell back as I shut the door. I turned and made my way out of my apartment building. Pulling my jacket closer around me, I called for a taxi.

When I got in a taxi, I stared out the window. Suddenly, a realization hit me. I left my phone at Ashton's! *Shit!* I didn't have time to go get it from him, and I didn't quite remember how to get back to his place. What also sucked was that I didn't know his number to call him and see if I could somehow meet up with him to get it. *Looks like I'm either going to have to buy a new phone or somehow reach Ashton to get mine back.* Sighing, I ran my hand over my ponytail. The taxi came to a stop outside of the restaurant The River Café. It was sort of small, but it had one of the best views in the whole city. It sat beside the river and overlooked the city from afar. It was a real romantic spot. I wished someone would bring me here.

The place was always busy, and people who had money or were celebrating a special occasion came here. I could never afford this place, even though I got thirty percent off. Smiling kindly at the taxi driver, I paid him and went toward the door. I took a deep breath and opened it and made my way toward the back room to put my stuff away and get my apron. Honestly, the cafe was a good place to work. They treated me somewhat right and paid pretty well. The only problem was the owner thought all the waitresses should look slutty, thinking that would draw more customers.

Grabbing my apron after putting my purse in my locker and locking it, I wrapped it around my waist and started for the kitchen. People scurried around the kitchen doing one thing or another. I instantly knew it was already busy and the lunch rush hadn't even started yet. Seeing one of my work friends, Riley, struggling with a tray of food, I rushed over to help.

"Let me help," I said, grabbing three plates.

"Thanks, Layla," she said, gratefully grabbing the remaining three.

"No problem. Let's get this out." She nodded and led the way out of the kitchen and into the dining room. People were seated in all the available seats and were chatting. Following Riley toward a table by the window, I stood to the side holding the plates as she laid them down for the right people. Smiling at me gratefully, she took the last plates from my hands and I turned to the front desk to see what my tables were tonight.

"Hey, Kayleen, what are my tables today?" I asked the hostess.

"Hey, Layla, glad you're here. We are packed today and it's only ten-thirty. You have tables three, five, seven, nine, eleven, and thirteen," she said, looking down at the charts. "Tables five, seven, and eleven were just seated a few minutes ago. The others are under Kim and Riley." Smiling in thanks, I hurried over to table five not wanting to make them wait any longer. We were pretty understaffed, so usually I had to take on about eight tables alone. Memorizing the tables I had, I plastered a smile as I got to the table.

"Hello. I'm going to be your waitress, Layla. What can I start you guys off with?" I asked, taking out my writing pad and pen. After the couple gave me their order, I hurried it back to the kitchen and went to my other tables getting their orders, drinks, and their checks.

Over the next hour or so I bounced between each table, the kitchen, and back. I didn't get a break and was constantly moving. Sometimes I wasn't even serving my tables but helping other waitresses carrying plates and stuff. Just as I was dropping an order off to the kitchen, Riley came over and told me Kayleen from the front desk was asking for me. Wondering what she needed, I made my way over there.

"You needed me?" I asked her once I got to the front.

"Layla, I need you to take table twenty-three out on the deck. No one else can take it," she told me hopefully.

"But I already have six tables," I protested slightly. It wasn't like I didn't want to take the table. It's just I was already busy and table twenty-three was outside and in a corner almost where no one could see it. It was of course one of the nicer views, so lovely-dovey couples liked that table. I couldn't count how many times I had gone out there to take orders only to find the couple in a heavy make-out session. And having to break them apart was not fun.

"Please? Riley just got done with one of her tables and said she can take one of yours," Kayleen said. With her looking at me with puppy dog eyes, I gave in. *Why do I have to be so nice?*

"Okay, fine. Table twenty-three, right?" I asked, wanting to make sure I got the right table. As she nodded, I sighed inwardly and made my way out the back doors that led to the outside deck. It was a nice day. The sun shone brightly, warming up my skin. I suppressed a sigh as I walked through the door.

If only I could be out soaking the sun instead of working. Making my way to the corner of the deck, I saw two males already sitting. The guy who had his back to me had wide shoulders, encased in a nice dark blue suit, and almost shaggy dark brown hair. The guy across from him was nice looking too. He had short hair that was blonde, and a well-defined jawline that I could see from here. He was also dressed in a nice suit that hugged his frame. *Great, I get the table with not one, but two possibly hot guys.* Walking over to the table, I smiled.

"Hello. How are you guys today? I'll be your server, Layla," I said, taking out my writing pad and pen then looking up at them. My breath caught in my throat. I stood there looking like a fish out of water with my mouth open. I didn't think I'd ever see him again, let alone see him this soon. Sitting in front of me was none other than Ashton.

***

Ashton

After getting dressed in a white shirt and a dark suit, I called for my car to be brought around out front. I had only thirty minutes to get to a meeting on the other side of the river. Straightening my tie, I grabbed my cellphone and Layla's.

When I had gotten done with working out, I was on my way to shower when I noticed a different cellphone next to mine. Confused, I picked it up and looked at it. It was an older model, whereas mine was the new one, and had a light blue case. *Definitely not mine, must be Layla's,* I thought. A small part of me almost jumped in excitement because having her cellphone meant I would have to see her again. Smirking at myself, I set the phone back down and headed to the shower. Once I had stripped, I stepped into the warm water.

The water cascaded down my back and soothed my tense muscles. After standing under the water for a good few minutes, I washed my hair and body, washing all the sweat off of me. After spending about ten minutes in the shower, I finally stepped out and wrapped a towel around me. When I looked in the mirror, I saw a man about twenty-five with shaggy dark brown hair that needed a cut, and a pair of steel-blue eyes that already had bags under them and stress lines around them. A light stubble grazed my jaw. I looked down to my chest and stomach. My body was well defined and an eight-pack reflected in the mirror. I looked older than I was, and I knew I worked harder than I should. I should be having more fun and stressing less, but working helped me and got my mind off certain things.

Looking at the clock, I saw I needed to get going. Walking into my huge walk-in closet, I went straight to my suits. I had a huge selection, but I grabbed a white button-up shirt, dark blue dress pants, and a dark blue tie to go with it. Straightening my tie and shirt sleeves, I pulled on the matching blue suit jacket. I went to the bathroom, brushed my teeth, and brushed my hair into place. When I got back into my room, I put on my Rolex, and grabbed my wallet and both Layla and I's phones. *I'll have to go by the office and see if I can get information on Layla,* I thought to myself as I made my way out of my apartment.

When I went down the elevator, it came to a stop at the bottom floor a minute later. Stepping out and through the front doors, I saw Clark there already with my car waiting for me. Nodding at him, I slipped through the open door and settled in as Clark shut the door behind me. The whole ride to the restaurant, I replayed everything I planned to say to Mike. He was planning on investing his millions in my company, and I needed to say the right things to get him to join. With him invested in me, hopefully some of his other rich friends would come on board as well. Being a millionaire at twenty-five made some people skeptical of me, mostly the older men with money. They didn't want some "kid" being trusted with their money. I could see what they meant, but if they ever took a glance at my records they would see how well I do, and that I'd make sure their money is well invested.

Clark pulled up in front of the restaurant in what

seemed like minutes. Checking my watch, I saw I was only a few minutes late—fashionably late, I'd like to call it. Being later than the company you're waiting for shows that you don't really care all that much, but in reality, you do. It's supposed to make that person think you have much more important things to deal with. It also helps if you add in, "Sorry I was late. I got stuck at the office going over files and such."

Stepping out of the vehicle, I nodded at Clark in thanks and walked into the restaurant. I liked to come to this place with future investors. It helped seal the deal with the view and the sexy waitresses. The moment I walked to the front desk, the woman there immediately straightened up. Smirking, I started talked to her.

"Hello. I already have a reservation. My other party may even be here. It's under Miller," I said, flashing her a smile girls drool over. Her cheeks turned red as she nodded and looked for my reservation on her computer.

"Uh, yes. Your party is already here waiting for you, Mr. Miller," she said, trying not to stutter. I took a brief glance around the restaurant and from the corner of my eye, I saw her pull her shirt down a tad bit more to show more cleavage. *Hmm, she doesn't look too bad. Maybe I'll have to get with her soon.* Seeing my eyes trailing to her breasts, she smiled and walked me out to my table on the deck facing the river. I saw Mike was already there and taking a sip of his drink. Smirking at the girl, I sneaked a hand around and grabbed her ass then sat down. She stood there flushed for a second then turned and left. Smiling inwardly, I turned to Mike.

"Hi Mike. Sorry I'm late. I got stuck at the office," I said, lying.

"No, that's fine," he said. Mike was about my age, maybe a little older. He had blonde hair that was short, and blue eyes. He was well built and could look intimidating when he wanted to. "Glad we could meet up."

"Same here. We have some things to discuss." Before I could say any more, a female voice interrupted me. The voice sounded oddly familiar. Turning, I came face-to-face with Layla.

Chapter 6

Layla

Seeing Ashton almost made me gasp. *What the hell is he doing here?* He just stared up at me. I saw the moment he went from surprise to amusement.

"Layla," he said, my name rolling off his tongue. I couldn't keep myself from liking how he said my name. He made it seem fancier or somehow sexier. All I could picture was us in bed together the night before. Not wanting to seem unprofessional since he had company, I decided to ignore him.

"Hi, I'll be your waitress. Anything I can start you off with?" I said, looking down at my pad not wanting to make eye contact with Ashton.

"Layla." He said my name again.

"Yes, what can I get you?" I asked, trying to ignore him. I could feel the other guy's gaze on me, and my cheeks flamed a pink color.

"You can't ignore me forever, Layla," Ashton said, and I could hear the smirk in his voice. *Well, I'm going to try.*

"What can I start you guys with?" I repeated. I heard a snort of laughter and looked up. The guy sitting with Ashton smiled at me and shook his head.

"Can I get another one?" the blonde guy asked, shaking his empty glass.

"Of course, what is it?" I asked.

"Vodka and tonic."

"And you?" I asked Ashton, daring a glance at him.

"Whiskey," Ashton said, looking at me. His bright blue eyes seemed to freeze me on the spot. He just stared at me until I felt my cheeks turn even redder.

"O-okay," I finally stuttered and looked away. I turned and made my way to the bar to get their drinks.

Layla, ignore him and don't let him get to you, I told myself as I waited for Ted, the bartender, to get the drinks. For some stupid reason, he just seemed to make my knees go weak. *You just like him because he saved you and he took care of you. Don't think about him and just serve him; then he'll be out if your life forever.* Grabbing the drinks, I headed back to the table. *You can do this, Layla. You can do this,* I chanted to myself. My legs were almost shaky as I walked back to the table with their drinks. I didn't know why I was nervous, but I couldn't seem to calm myself down. Maybe it was because I thought I would never see Ashton again and that I now know he was a millionaire and self-proclaimed womanizer, but who knew.

"Here you go," I said, putting the drinks down

for them. "You guys ready to order?" I asked, trying to steady my voice. Thankfully, it came out stronger than I thought. *You can do this, Layla. You are not weak.*

"Yes, I'll have the blackened salmon with asparagus," the blonde guy said, smiling at me while handing me his menu. The guy was super cute. His blonde hair was short but it seemed to fit him, and his blue eyes stared back at me almost with a twinkle. He may have been slightly older than me, maybe seven years, but he didn't look too bad.

"Okay," I said, smiling back. There was one perk to working here: there were plenty of cute guys. "And you?"

"I'll have the shrimp stir fry," Ashton said. He handed me his menu but made sure his hand touched mine and lingered. Taking a deep breath, I forced a smile on my face.

"I'll get that in for you," I said then hurried and turned around. I ignored how my skin tingled at his touch, and dropped the order off at the kitchen and made my way around to my other tables. The whole time I kept telling myself, *Just do your job. Ignore him and just serve him his food like the lower-class person you are.* After I said that, I frowned at myself. *Great, Layla, make yourself feel worse than you already are. But it's true.* Shaking my head at myself, I went back to Ashton's table to see if they needed anything.

I straightened my skirt unconsciously. I could see Ashton was laughing at something the other man said because his wide shoulders shook. From here, I could hear Ashton's laugh and I instantly wanted to hear it again. It was a deep laugh; if only I were in front of him admiring the smile that was probably on his face. The guy across from him had a smile on his face and laughed as well. I cleared my throat as I stood by the side of the table, not wanting to scare them nor interrupt their conversation.

"Hi. You guys need anything?" I asked.

"Can I get a refill?" the blonde guy asked again. I smiled and nodded. I looked over at Ashton, but he shook his head. Turning, I went and got the refill. Just as I was heading to take it back, I heard the bell ring for Ashton's order. Glad, I hurried back to the table and dropped off the drink. They seemed to ignore me and looked to be in deep, serious conversation. I made my way back to the kitchen and grabbed both of their dishes. Balancing the two in my hands, I weaved around tables and to the deck.

"Okay, here you go. Here is the blackened salmon with asparagus," I said, holding Ashton's plate in one hand and setting the blonde guy's down in front of him. "And here is the shrimp stir fry." I sat his down and wiped my hands on my apron. "Need anything else?" I asked.

"No, I think we are good. Thank you, Layla," Ashton said, his voice deep and smooth like honey. I smiled and left to my other tables. It was kind of weird having Ashton see me like this. He probably thought I was low class and now regretted helping me.

I went back and forth between tables and the

kitchen constantly. The restaurant was getting busier and louder. I already handed Ashton and the guy their bills before going to help my other tables. With my tables content for the next little bit, I made my way back outside to see if Ashton was done. When I walked out there, I found no one. Both chairs were pushed in and empty plates littered the table. Their bills were on the edge of the table. For some reason, a wave of sadness crashed over me. Ashton left without saying anything to me. *Why would he, Layla? You're nothing but trash to him anyways.* Clenching my jaw, I picked up their bills and opened each of them.

Instantly, my eyes widened. They both left a *big* tip, and by big I meant one hundred dollars from each. Wow! That was a lot; that more than I sometimes got on most nights. I was even lucky to just get twenty bucks when someone was feeling generous or when the holidays came around. Shocked, I made my way back inside I put the one hundred-dollar bills in my pocket. I spent the rest of the night going from table to table, to the bar, and to the kitchen. Finally, five o'clock came and I could leave. I waved bye to everyone and grabbed my stuff, ready to get the hell out of here. As I stepped out of the door, I breathed in the semi-clean air. The air smelled like the ocean, fresh and salty. The sun was still up, and I was glad it was still a combination of summer and early fall. It wasn't cold or too hot, just perfect outside. Just glad to be done with work, I walked to the curb ready to hail a taxi. Just as I was putting up my hand to get a taxi, a car horn sounded right by me scaring the shit out of me.

Jumping, I turned around and saw a black limo idling on the curb. *What the*—I stared at the car as fear slowly crept into me. *Who is in the car?* When an unknown car pulls up near you, you know it isn't for a good reason. And last night had me jumpier than usual. I narrowed my eyes trying to not look scared. The door opened and out stepped none other than Ashton Miller.

Chapter 7

Layla

Seeing Ashton stepping out of the car, a wave of relief washed over me. *Thank god, it's only him*, I thought.

"Ashton! You scared the shit out of me!" I yelled at him. I heard a deep chuckle escape him as he walked toward me.

"That's how you treat someone who helped you last night?" he said as he came to a stop in front of me. I had to tilt my head up just to see his face, he was that much taller than me. I looked him over and saw he had removed his suit jacket and was just wearing a white button-up shirt with the sleeves rolled up, and no tie. He was actually very sexy— sexier than when he was fully dressed up in his suit and tie. At the mention of last night, I couldn't stop the shiver that ran down my back. He must have noticed, because he came a step closer.

"I've taken it as my duty to make sure you get home safely," Ashton said. I couldn't help but scoff.

"It isn't your 'duty.' I'll be fine on my own," I said, defending myself.

"Yeah, right. One second you're by yourself, and then you're being surrounded by a group of men. So, no, you won't be fine on your own," he said.

"You don't even know me. Why are you talking as if you know me?" I asked, cocking my hip and putting my hand on it. He stared at me.

"Do you want a ride or not?" he snapped.

Whoa, what suddenly crawled up his ass? I stared at him debating if I should get in the car with him. For one, I didn't know him at all, even though I'd "slept" with him last night, and second, I barely found out he was a multimillionaire, and third…well, I didn't really have a third. A small part of me wanted to get in the car. *Kacey is always telling me to do something fun and be carefree for once, so maybe I should. You don't know what it could lead to.* Biting my lip, I glanced around. Before I could think about it anymore, I opened my mouth.

"Okay." I was shocked the moment the word left my lips. Apparently so was he, because he stood still for a second, surprise on his face.

"Okay, let's go," he said, clearing his throat.

I followed behind him as he walked to the back of the car. As we got closer, I saw the outline of a guy in the driver's seat. *Ashton has a driver? Really?* He opened the door behind the driver's side. Smiling in thanks, I slid inside, trying to do it gracefully and not flash him unwanted skin. Now that would be embarrassing. When I slid all the way over, Ashton came in after me, sitting next to me. I looked around the limo and tried hard not to stare like a weirdo. I'd never been in a limo, but I didn't want Ashton thinking I was a weirdo or giving him more reason to think I was low class.

"You have a driver," I said to him.

"Yes. This is Clark. He is my main driver and bodyguard," Ashton said, nodding to Clark. Clark had dark brown hair and didn't look a day over thirty. He was kind of scary, but when he flashed me a small smile, I smiled back, not feeling scared about him. He was probably one of those guys who looked scary but were really big softies.

"Hi Clark," I said, nodding in greeting.

"So, you want to go home?" Ashton asked.

"Yeah, where else would I go?" I said in a "duh" tone.

"With me to my place," he said immediately, sending me a smirk.

"You wish." *Yeah, Layla, just play it off.* Instead of replying, he just sat there staring at me. Silence wrapped itself around us. The only sound that could be heard was the engine. "What?" I finally snapped, hating the silence and his stare. His blue eyes seemed to see my soul and everything buried under it, like he could see my demons.

"I need your address to get you home," Ashton said calmly. I blushed and looked down at my hands.

"Sorry. It's 225 Thornley Avenue, right by Kelly's Bookstore and Coffee Shop," I said. Ashton nodded then leaned to tell Clark the directions. I could see Clark nod, then the car started forward. Ashton turned back around and looked at me.

"Thank you," I said quietly, feeling embarrassed and somewhat shy.

We sat in silence as the car moved down the street toward downtown New York. Even though I'd lived here my whole life, heading downtown and seeing all the tall buildings and shops on the road somehow made me excited, and had me looking out the window like a five-year-old. We drove over the bridge making our way into downtown.

"So, have you always lived here?" Ashton asked me suddenly.

"Uh, yes," I said, looking back at him. "You?"

"Yeah, I have. It's my home town." He smiled out the window.

"Mine too."

Once again, silence laced itself around us. It wasn't uncomfortable silence though. For some strange reason, it felt right and easy being around Ashton. Yep, I'd either become crazy or was losing my mind. I hadn't even known him a full day yet and here I was, inside his car and feeling as if it were right to be doing so. If this were like any regular day, I would be in a cab heading home while Ashton would either be at work or taking "home" one of his many girls. I've heard enough about him through the news, aka Kacey, about his little 'escapades' with plenty of girls. Hell, he was the most eligible bachelor in New York for crying out loud. It's no wonder he had plenty of girls hanging off his arm.

We stayed silent as Clark drove through the traffic and toward my apartment. The sun was starting to set; it was about twenty after five. Finally, I saw my street and the car came to a stop. I looked up at my building feeling sad that I had to leave.

"Well, this is me," I said, turning to Ashton to thank him. "Thank you for the ride."

"You're welcome. Oh, wait, I have something for you," Ashton said, reaching into his pockets and pulling something out. "I believe this belongs to you." He held out my cellphone.

"You had it? Thank you!" I said, surprised. I thought I wouldn't be able to get it back from him. I gently took it from his hand, my fingertips grazing his fingers. There was something about his touch that made my skin tingle and feel all fuzzy. He was like a battery, and when you touched it you felt a small spark along your skin.

"Yeah. You left it at my apartment this morning in your rush," he said, shooting me a smile.

"Sorry about that." I blushed. "I didn't think you'd want me hanging around when you got up, so I hurried and left."

"It's fine. But you owe me." He smirked.

"Owe you?"

"Yes. I took care of you and you didn't even stick around so yes, you owe me. You owe me a date."

"I—uh, what?"

"Yes. I'll let you know when. Now get your fine ass out. I got meetings to go to." He made a shooing motion with his hands.

"You serious?" I said, shooting him a glare.

"Yes." The door opened and Clark stood just

beside it, waiting for me. I turned and looked back at Ashton and shook my head. *He's so weird.* "Bye, Layla," he said as I slid out the car.

"Bye," I called back and thanked Clark. All he did was nod. It was weird that I'd seen him multiple times, but he hadn't said a single word. I watched as the car drove away, and started to smile. That was the weirdest car ride to say the least. I turned and made my way up to my apartment with a smile on my face.

I made my way up the stairs thinking about Ashton the entire time. My mind wouldn't shut up for some reason and it was starting to make me worry. *Why am I suddenly thinking about him? Hell, why am I thinking about guys in general?* It had been ingrained in my head that I would never find someone, and that I was never good enough. So, thinking about a guy should be the last thing I was doing. It seemed Ashton had a hold on my brain and I wouldn't be able to shake him off anytime soon.

"Is that you, Layla?" called Kacey.

"Yeah," I called back, setting my apron and keys on the table we had by the front door.

"How was work?"

"It was okay," I said, debating with myself if I should tell her that I had to help Ashton and got a ride from him. *She's your best friend. You have to tell her.* "I have something to tell you," I said finally, walking into the kitchen and finding her leaning back up from the fridge with a tub of cookie dough in her hand. That was another reason her and me were best friends. We both loved cookie dough with a passion and thought it was a major food group.

"What is it? Did you do something wrong?" she accused as she grabbed two spoons and walked past me to the couch.

"No! It's not something bad. And I didn't do anything!" I took a seat next to her and grabbed the spoon she held out to me. Taking a deep breath, I told her all about this afternoon.

"What?" she yelled, practically jumping up and waving her spoon full of cookie dough. "You served him then got a ride home from him! How sweet of him to offer." She made an aww face and smiled at me.

"I guess. He was probably just doing it because he felt bad about what happened last night," I reasoned, digging my spoon in for some more cookie dough. I took a bite almost angrily because I didn't want it to be true, but I knew it was.

"Yeah, right. I think he likes you."

"No, he doesn't. He just feels responsible or something."

"He saved your phone and gave it back to you. He waited until you were off to give you a ride. If it were me, I would have thrown your phone away and left the minute I was done eating. I wouldn't wait for your sorry ass," Kacey said.

"Aw thanks, Kacey. It's great knowing how much you love me," I said sarcastically. She just smiled at me.

"He likes you. Try and deny it but I know you hope he does!" she said, shooting me a pointed look.

"I…never mind. I'm not getting into this. Let's just watch *Pretty Little Liars*."

She held her hands up in surrender and leaned back into the couch. For the next hour, we sat on our couch watching *Pretty Little Liars* and eating more cookie dough then should be allowed. The sound of my phone beeping from a text made me get up and grab it. Jumping back onto the couch, I looked down and almost gasped and laughed at the same time.

Sexy Beast (Ashton): Layla, I am picking you up tomorrow at nine a.m. sharp. Dress comfortable and sexy. ;) Don't think about me too much tonight. See you tomorrow.

"What? Who's it from?" Kacey asked, leaning over me to see. "Ashton texted you! And he wants to see you tomorrow, and he added his name into your phone!" she said rapidly.

"Kacey, breathe," I said

"This is great! Layla, you have a date with a *hot millionaire*!" Kacey screamed. I leaned away from her wanting to protect my eardrums.

"It's not a date! He just wants to see me or something," I said, trying to play it off like it was no big deal even though it was. On the outside, I was calm, but on the inside, I was freaking out.

"Layla, you will not ruin this for me! You are going on a date with Ashton! We need to figure out what you're going to wear." She got up and grabbed my hand, dragging me toward my bedroom.

I would be lying if I said I was actually looking

forward to tomorrow. I, Layla Kingston, am going on a date with a *hot* multimillionaire.

Chapter 8

Layla

The next morning, I found myself standing in front of my mirror with Kacey next to me. My floor was littered with every single piece of clothing I had, as was my bed. I looked at myself in the mirror.

"I don't think so," I said. Kacey had picked out a dress for me to wear. It was super cute, but it seemed too fancy or like I was trying too hard. Ashton said to dress comfortable but sexy. *How the hell am I supposed to do that?* "It looks like I'm trying too hard, Kacey."

"No, it doesn't," she protested, turning to me.

"Yes, it does. Let's look for something different."

I turned and went to look through my clothes for something better. After a few minutes of not finding anything, I grabbed my phone sending a text to Ashton to see what exactly we were doing.

To: Sexy Beast (Ashton)

From: Layla
It's Layla. What are we doing today?

I stood by my bed looking over my clothes and suddenly my phone beeped in my hands. Looking down, I saw it was a reply from Ashton.

From: Sexy Beast (Ashton)
To: Layla
Nothing extreme. Probably lunch and something else.

Like that helps, I thought sarcastically. The sound of my name being called had my head snapping toward Kacey.

"I found the perfect outfit," she said, holding up a pair of dark-washed jeans and a white sweater.

"Okay." I grabbed them and started taking off my clothes. Kacey and I had seen each other practically naked, so it wasn't uncomfortable to get undressed in front of her. I stood there in my bra and panties reaching for the jeans. Since they were black skinny jeans, I had to do the little dance to just put them on. I reached for the sweater. As I reached for the sweater, I saw Kacey's eyes on my stomach. I knew what she was looking at.

Across my stomach from my left side of my ribs to just above my belly button was a jagged scar. Just looking at it made me sick. Not wanting to look at it and remember how I got it, I pulled the sweater quickly over it. Kacey sent me an apologetic look, but I waved her off. I didn't blame her for staring at it, even I couldn't look at it too long and it'd been two years since I got it.

"Yes, that's the outfit. But it needs something," Kacey said, looking around my room. A second later, she held up a pair of high-heeled black booties with a peep toe. I couldn't help but smile. Slipping them on, I smiled at her.

"I like it," I said. The outfit was plain and simple, but also kind of fancy.

"Yes, you look hot but let's hurry and do something with your hair."

"Hey! My hair looks fine!" I said defensively.

"Okay. Sit." She pointed at the chair in front of my desk and mirror.

Obeying her, I took a seat and let her do her work. Honestly, Kacey could do wonders on anyone. I closed my eyes and let her do her thing as she pulled my hair and poked my eyes with eyeliner. I kept protesting why I needed to be all pretty and dressed up, and all she would tell me was that I was going on a date with a millionaire and I couldn't show up looking like a hobo. Yep, my best friend sure knew how to make me feel good.

"There you go," she announced proudly. Opening my eyes, I stared at myself. I couldn't help but smile at my reflection. Kacey didn't do a lot; she just added enough to highlight my features and make it look natural. My gray eyes popped as Kacey put some eyeliner and mascara on them. Silvery eye shadow also made them pop. A little bit of blush covered my cheeks. My lips were covered in a pale shade of pink. My brown hair hung down in soft waves, and a piece was pulled to the side and clipped at the back of my head. The look was completely me and I loved that Kacey did it that way.

"I love it. Thank you, Kay!" I said, standing up and hugging her.

"You're welcome. You look smoking hot. Ashton won't know what hit him." I smiled at her and grabbed the small shoulder bag on my bed. I put my wallet, keys, some extra lipstick, and gum inside. I grabbed my phone and checked it to make sure I'd didn't miss a text.

"When you get home, I expect a full report on what happened, what you did. So basically, everything that happens from the moment you leave here until you step back into the apartment. Got it?" Kacey told me, her voice hard and commanding.

"Yes, Mom, I promise," I said, smiling at her. Even though she could be demanding and sometimes pushy, I loved her to death. I didn't think I'd be here or want to be here if she weren't. I'm just glad she's my best friend and hasn't ever left me. "Thank you for doing my hair and makeup." I hugged her tightly.

"You're welcome. Someone's got to make sure you live and look amazing. Because without me, you wouldn't be able to live or look good," she said.

"Awww, it wouldn't be a good day without you saying I'm pretty without your help," I said sarcastically.

"Someone's got to do it," she said, smiling at me. Laughing, I shook my head at her. Just then, my phone buzzed. I saw it was Ashton.

"Okay, I gotta go. See you later," I said, pulling my bag onto my shoulder.

"Okay. See you later. Have fun if he invites you back to his apartment." She winked at me.

"Kacey!" I said.

"What? Just go." She opened the door and shoved me out. "Have fun! Use protection!" With that, she shut the door on me. Great.

I walked down the stairs and outside. Idling by the curb was Ashton's limo. The moment I stepped out of doors, I saw Ashton step out of the limo and come toward me. His driver stood off to the side with the door still open, waiting for us.

"Layla," he said a smirk as he stopped in front of me, his toes touching mine. I strained my neck up at him.

"Ashton," I said, my voice kind of shaky. *Layla, you got this, act cool. Don't let him know how he affects you.* "I gotta say…you look very hot today." He looked me up and down. I could practically see him undressing me in his head.

"I know I do. I thought I may see some attractive guys while we are out." I smirked at him and walked toward the car, leaving him standing there with a weird look mixed with surprise and anger. Smiling and nodding in thanks to the driver. I slid inside. A second later, Ashton slid in beside me. By his posture, I could tell he was angry for some reason. *Doesn't he know I was joking?*

The car started forward and we sat in silence. Ashton stared out the window and I sat there playing with the rings I had put on at the last moment. I was usually fine with silence, but for some reason, I couldn't stand another second of sitting here with awkward silence wrapped around us.

"So where are we going?" I finally asked, biting my bottom lip hoping Ashton would answer.

"Somewhere," he answered vaguely.

"Great answer. That really helps," I said sarcastically, looking out the opposite window. We rode in silence as we got deeper into the city. I almost felt like a tourist as I leaned against the window to look outside more easily. New York had always fascinated me, even as a child. I was never allowed to come downtown like most kids in high school. Even after living here for four years, I still have not shopped or looked around in downtown New York. I never had the time or the money to do so. Kacey always invites me to come with her, but I'm either working, have class, or just too broke. So now I was looking at everything I could as the limo driver maneuvered us around traffic.

"Whoa," I breathed as we passed the jumbo-sized TV's playing ads, the big posters announcing upcoming movies, and the big crowd surrounding a building for what looked like the *Good Morning America* set. I felt like a child seeing candy for the first time, and I couldn't seem to stop myself from taking everything in. "It's so pretty," I murmured after we had passed it all. *I bet it is as pretty at night with all the lights going.*

"Have you never seen downtown New York before?" Ashton asked softly next to me. A blush erupted across my cheeks before I could stop it. I looked over at him sheepishly, not having realized I was acting like a weirdo.

"I-I haven't before." I finally stuttered out. God,

what was wrong with me? Layla, get yourself together!

"You've lived here your whole life but you haven't seen downtown?" he asked, confused.

"Well, I lived about twenty minutes outside of town and my parents were...strict," I replied vaguely. I'd really only seen downtown New York briefly once or twice, when Kacey made me go to a party with her at night.

He sat there quietly, a strange look on his face. Not even a minute later, he smirked to himself and turned back to me. I looked at him confused, but also curious. *What was he thinking about?* I wondered. Before we could say anything, the limo came to a stop. I tried glancing out the window behind Ashton's head, but I couldn't see anything. The door opened up not even a second later. Ashton stepped out of the limo then turned, holding a hand out for me. I slid over and tried to gracefully step out like Ashton did, but instead almost ended up tripping. Ashton's warm hand gripped my hand, preventing me from embarrassing myself. A blush crept onto my face and I looked anywhere but at him.

"Thank you," I said. I started taking in the place. In front of me was what looked like an expensive restaurant. Couples and business partners sat outside enjoying the semi-cold air and talking to one another. A slight tug on my arm alerted me that the front door to the restaurant was being held open for us. Ashton tugged me along behind him as we walked through and to the front counter.

"Hello, Mr. Miller," a tall blonde purred at

Ashton. I looked up at her and scowled. And I thought my uniform was small; this woman's top was so tight you could see the outline of her bra. Her breasts were practically pushed up to her ears and looked ready to fall with a deep breath. I didn't even want to know what bottoms she was wearing. Her face was caked in makeup, and I could see her hair was dyed that ugly blonde color. Her blue eyes didn't even glance in my direction as she stared at Ashton as if he were a piece of meat. "Would you like a table outside or inside?" she asked, her voice coming out all nasally.

"A table outside please," he said, not really making eye contact with her. She seemed surprised for a second, but recovered and grabbed a menu and turned to lead us to our table. Noticing that she grabbed just one, I rolled my eyes and snatched a menu off the counter before following after Ashton. As I trailed behind them, I saw she kept pressing herself against his side. A part of me wanted to walk right up to her and rip her fake blonde hair out. Shocked at myself, I shook my head. *Why does it even matter to me? It's not like we are dating. Yes, but you are out on a date with him and she's practically on top of him, oblivious to you.* 'We finally reached our table and the girl pressed herself close to Ashton as she set his menu on the table.

"If you need anything, just let me know." She winked at him and bounced off. Rolling my eyes, I sat down in my chair.

"I was going to hold your chair out for you," Ashton said next to me.

"I got it," was all I said. I heard him sigh and I

smiled inwardly. I wouldn't be some damsel in distress around Ashton. I can handle things myself and have for years now. *But he helped you the other night,* a voice reasoned in the back of my mind. Before I could argue, Ashton asked me something. "Hmmm?" I asked, not hearing what he said.

"What do you like to eat? This place has a good selection." He glanced up at me over his menu.

"I like almost anything, just not seafood." Something about the texture has always bothered me.

"You don't like seafood?" Ashton practically gasped at me. I couldn't help but laugh softly at his expression. He almost looked like I had kicked a puppy or something.

"No. It just tastes weird to me," I said, shrugging.

"I don't know who you are." He shook his head at me but when he looked up, his eyes were filled with amusement.

"Not liking seafood isn't as bad as not liking cookie dough," I said.

"I don't like cookie dough." I gasped, not believing my ears.

"You don't like cookie dough?"

"Nope." He shrugged just like I had.

"What kind of person are you?" Ashton just stared at me in amusement.

"What's the big deal? It's just cookie dough. I'd rather eat it after it's been cooked." I just shook my head at him and looked down at my menu.

To say this was a fancy would be an understatement. The meals were pretty pricey. A plate of pasta was close to thirty bucks. *That better be some damn good pasta.* I looked for the cheapest thing to get and only ended up with a side salad for close to ten dollars. Ashton must have seen the look on my face.

"Layla, don't worry about the price. I'm paying," he said.

"Have you not seen these prices? They are more than my paychecks."

"I can afford it. It's okay get whatever you want." I really wanted to say "'yeah, I know,'" but I held it in until after we ordered to hound him as to why he didn't tell me he was a millionaire. A few minutes later, a waitress came over to get out drink order.

"Hello, what can I get you two to drink?" she asked. She was really pretty with short brown hair and light green eyes, and her name tag read Amy. When she smiled down at us, I saw she wasn't looking at Ashton like the other girls. Shooting her a smile, I answered.

"I'll just have water."

"Same here," Ashton said as well.

"Okay. Are you ready to order or need a few minutes?" Ashton looked at me silently. Nodding, he turned to Amy.

"I'll have the lasagna with garlic bread." He handed her his menu.

"I'll have the pasta marinara and garlic bread also." I smiled and handed her my menu as well. Might as well let him pay for my expensive meal. A slight payback for not telling me he had money.

"Sounds good. I'll hurry and get that in and get

you your drinks."

After she left, we sat in silence. I could feel his gaze on me, making me feel self-conscious.

"So, are you in college still?" he asked, breaking the silence.

"No, I finished almost two years ago."

"Oh, where did you go? NYU?"

"Yeah, me and my friend Kacey both got in."

"She's the one from the club, right?" I couldn't help but be surprised that he remembered Kacey from the other night. I nodded and not even a second later, our waters were placed in front of us. "What did you study and major in?"

"I studied English and majored in Journalism. I want to be a writer or an editor," I said, taking a sip of my water. He actually looked impressed. "How about you? What did you study?" I asked, wanting to know more about him.

"I went to NYU too and majored in Business."

"That's pretty cool. Is that how you got your company started?" Ashton seemed to be surprised for a second before answering.

"How did you know?" he asked.

"You're all over the internet and magazines. Did you think I wouldn't find out?" I asked, giving him a look.

"Well, I guess you would have found out sooner or later anyways. It's no big deal."

"No big deal? You're a multi-millionaire." He just shrugged.

"Yes, but it doesn't matter. I leave business at work. I don't bring it into my personal affairs." His voice was serious, almost like a warning.

"That's good. No one likes talking business when they are on a date anyways," I said, letting him know I was not going to go picking around in his business. What he did on his own time was his business, not mine. He seemed happy after I said that and sent me a smirk. But this time the smirk wasn't cocky; it was just a smirk, almost a smile.

We sat there and talked for about five minutes about nothing in particular, before our meals came. When mine was placed in front of me, I was happy to know that it was actually a big portion instead of a small one. My stomach growled softly and I put a hand on it, trying to silence it. My pasta looked and smelled amazing, but Ashton's lasagna looked great too. Grabbing my fork, I took a bite. I couldn't stop a small moan from escaping my lips. The pasta tasted like something you'd get in Italy.

"Good?" Ashton asked, smirking at me in amusement. I nodded and felt my cheeks heat up.

While we were eating, I couldn't help but glance up at Ashton. He looked like a model who just stepped out of a magazine. I couldn't help but think that this date was going to turn out amazing.

Chapter 9

Layla

After we had finished eating and got the check, we made our way back to the car. I felt bad having Ashton pay, but after being firmly told he got it I backed off. I was now back inside the limo driving to god knows where. Ashton sat quietly next to me, occasionally tapping away at his phone. I took that time that he wasn't looking at me to study him. To say he was hot was an understatement. He was beyond gorgeous. His brown hair was in a messy but sexy style. His dark blue suit looked great on him, but on anyone else, it would have looked funny. It made his blue eyes pop out even more. The suit jacket hugged his wide muscular shoulders and highlighted his strong arms. The jacket looked almost like the seams would burst free by his large biceps. And don't get me started on the slacks that hugged his well-toned backside. There was something about a man in a suit that made a woman weak in the knees.

Ashton's well-defined jaw clenched as he read something on his phone. I couldn't help but feel turned on by that. His fingers flew across his phone, and I wondered what was going on. The longer I stared at him, the more I wondered why he asked me out. *Maybe out of pity?* I wouldn't lie that just the thought of that hurt. Before I could depress myself, I felt my phone buzz in my bag. Reaching in, I saw I got a text from Kacey.

To: Layla
From: Kacey (the emoji of a crown)
How's your date going? Did you decide to skip lunch and go straight to dessert?

I instantly felt my cheeks heat up. Only Kacey would think that.

To: Kacey
From: Layla
NO! Why would you think that?

Not even a second later, she replied. I could tell she was waiting by her phone waiting for my reply.

To: Layla
From: Kacey
What? He's hot. You should shag him before it's too late.

After reading her text, I quickly turned off my phone not bothering to reply. Of course, Kacey would tell me to sleep with the most eligible bachelor in New York; someone who is also the biggest player around. After putting my phone away, I looked up as I felt the car coming to a stop. Glancing out the window, I didn't recognize where we were.

"Ashton, where are we?" I finally asked.

"It's a surprise," he said as his driver opened the door for us. I slid out and stepped to the side, waiting for Ashton to come out. I glanced around trying to figure out where we were, but with no such luck. After Ashton thanked his driver, he put a hand on my lower back.

"Let's go," was all he said, nudging me forward toward a big building.

As we walked toward the building, I couldn't help but wonder where we were. After Ashton held the door open for me, I slid inside and glanced around. I instantly started to recognize where we were. Posters of all different kinds of sea life covered the walls, and little kids ran around their parents as they left. Ashton had brought me to the aquarium. I have never been but have always wanted to go. I turned to Ashton with wide eyes.

"The aquarium!" I said, smiling.

"Yeah, I thought maybe you'd like it," Ashton mumbled, rubbing the back of his neck. Seeing him look almost embarrassed, I knew he didn't do this often.

"I love it." I looked around and saw the entrance that led deeper. "Let's go!" I said, grabbing his arm and pulling him to the entrance. I heard him chuckle as I dragged him. I came to a stop at the ticket booth reaching into my bag to grab my wallet. Just as I pulled out my wallet, a big hand was placed above mine stopping me.

"I got it." I started to protest but Ashton had already handed money over, and the lady was handing him our passes for inside. Glaring at the back of his head, I followed him inside not wanting to hold the line up.

"Ashton, I could have paid," I said.

"Yes, but I asked you out so I will be paying," he said firmly as he turned around to face me. Seeing his blue eyes staring down at me made my knees weak. I just nodded, not trusting myself to talk. *Layla, what's wrong with you?* I shouted at myself inside my head. *You're letting him get to you!*

"What do you want to see first?"

"Uh…I…um," I stuttered. I looked around and saw there were three hallways: one leading to the right, one to the left, and one straight ahead. "Let's go right," I said, hoping the hallways just linked together. Ashton nodded at me and we both started down the right hallway.

We were silent as we came up to the first display of sea animals. I saw all different kinds and colors of fish. There were orange, red, blue, yellow, brown, and even green fish!

"Look, there's Dory!" I said, pointing.

"Dory?" Ashton asked, confusion clear in his voice. I turned to him, resisting the urge to gasp.

"Dory? From *Finding Nemo*?"

"No, haven't heard of that. Is that a movie?"

"Yeah, it's an animated movie. Can't believe you've never seen or even heard of it."

"I've been too busy working to watch some kid

movie."

"It's not just a kid movie! It's also an adult one. It's funny and has a life lesson." I needed to defend one of my favorite Disney movies.

"A life lesson? And what is that life lesson?" Ashton asked as we made our way slowly down the hallway.

"Well, the story is about a fish, Nemo, that gets kidnapped by humans and is taken to a doctor's office to be given as a gift. His dad, Marlin, goes out and tries to find him meeting all different kinds of sea life like a turtle, a shark, and Dory. Well, long story short, the lesson is that it's okay to get out of your comfort zone, and that it's okay to let someone or something you love go and let them find their own way," I said, looking at the fishes swimming around in their tank. Dory's quote, "Just keep swimming, just keep swimming," ran through my head. The sound of my heels clicking against the tile was the only sound that could be heard. Ashton was silent as we continued walking thinking about what I said.

"Well, that's...insightful," Ashton finally said. I couldn't help but snort at his response.

"It's a good movie. One day I'll get you to watch it." I nodded at my goal. From the corner of my eye, I saw Ashton just smirking.

"What are you, seven?" Ashton said not even a minute later.

"Hey, a twenty-three-year-old can watch a Disney movie," I said. He just rolled his eyes at me but dropped it.

The further we moved into the building, the

more fish we saw. It was probably weird seeing a man in a suit and a girl dressed up walking around a family attraction. We looked so out of place, but thankfully the aquarium wasn't busy today and it was only us. A few minutes later, we turned and walked under this glass fixture that let the fish swim over us. I looked up just in time to see a huge shark swim over us.

"Whoa! Look at that!" I said amazed as I tugged on Ashton's arm. I watched what I thought was a bullhead shark pass over us. Even though we were inside, its shadow passed over us, making it seem eerie. "That's a big shark."

We stood under it for a little while longer, watching all different kinds of fish go over us. As I watched them swim, I couldn't help but think how simple their lives were. All they did was swim around in their tank and didn't have to worry about being eaten, not being fed, or have to worry about anything. I couldn't help but think life would be so much simpler if we were fishes in a tank. We wouldn't have to worry about work, money, family, nothing other than ourselves. It would be so nice to swim and forget about everything. I felt a soft nudge on my hip, knocking me out of my thoughts.

"Did you see that one?" Ashton asked, pointing to a puffer fish. It was the same one from *Finding Nemo*; when you touch it, it puffs up.

"That one is cool. If you could be any fish or sea life, what would it be?" I asked, glancing up at him as we slowly walked. Ashton was silent as he thought over my question.

"I would be a shark," he said, and just then a big

white shark swam by.

"A shark, really?"

"Yes. They are the predators of the sea, along with whales. I'd rather be the king of the sea instead of a jellyfish or something," he reasoned.

"Typical guy response." I rolled my eyes.

"Okay fine, then what would you choose?"

"I'd choose a dolphin."

"That's such a woman response." He threw my words back at me.

"Okay, fine! It is, but dolphins are the kindest sea animals and are very smart."

"Sharks eat dolphins," Ashton pointed out.

"No, they don't. Dolphins don't get eaten!"

I turned and stared at him before starting to laugh. Two twenty-somethings arguing over stupid sea creatures, and one of them a famous CEO at that. Ashton just looked down at me like I was crazy.

"W-we are arguing like six-year-olds," I choked out, trying to suppress my laughter. Looking up at Ashton's confused face, I let my laughter burst free, echoing off the walls and down the hallway. "We are so w-weird!"

"I am not weird; that is you," Ashton said as I continued laughing for no real reason. My laughter slowly started to die down, and Ashton stood waiting for me to stop with a raised eyebrow.

"Sorry, that was just too funny," I finally said, calming down.

"You sure are a weird one," was all Ashton said as he walked ahead. I just smirked at his back. Being called weird was nothing compared to what

I've been called before. I honestly didn't mind being called weird.

I quickly caught up with Ashton, and we walked all around the aquarium making small talk. About twenty minutes later, I pulled Ashton to a stop in front of an open water tank. Inside swam little stingrays, starfish lay at the bottom and along the sides, and even little sharks were swimming around. A young-looking guy maybe my age or younger walked our way.

"Hello. This is our touching exhibit. You can reach in and touch any of the animals if you'd like."

"Is that safe? Won't the stingrays sting me or the shark bite me?" I asked, looking at his name tag, Terry. He shot me a pretty smile.

"No, it's perfectly safe. Come here." He gestured for me to come closer to the tank. Hesitantly, I walked over to his side. "Just reach your hand like this and they will just swim by." He laid his hand into the water only a few inches in. A second later, a stingray swam under his hand and his fingers grazed its back.

He looked back up at me smiling. Biting my bottom lip, I got closer, pulled my sleeve up, and slowly put my hand into the water just like Terry did. I saw a small shark making its way toward me and almost pulled my hand away when I felt a hand on my arm. I looked up and saw Ashton standing very close to me with his chest pressing into me back. He nodded at me encouragingly as the shark got closer. Smiling at him, I waited as the shark passed under my hand and I felt his slick skin. My grin got wider as I turned and looked up at Ashton.

"Did you see that?" I asked excitedly, not caring that I sounded like a five-year-old. I watched as a smile spread across Ashton's face. I grabbed his hand, wanting him to feel it too. His hand stopped me and I thought he would tell me to stop, but I was surprised to watch him shrug off his suit jacket and roll up his shirt sleeve. He grabbed my wet hand in his and dunked both of our hands under the water. I looked up at him, amazed that a guy like him was spending his day with someone like me. Here was a handsome, smart, and slightly famous, and I was just an average woman with no good looks, and a messed-up past, even though he didn't know that. I felt his hand nudge mine underwater, and I turned back to the tank. Coming toward us was both a stingray and a shark. Feeling their almost slimy skin, I couldn't help but smile.

I looked to my left and saw a starfish stuck to the side of the wall. I moved away from Ashton and toward the starfish. Reaching my hand in, I felt the rough skin and watched as it moved slightly. I've always liked starfish and here I was, touching one. I felt eyes on my back, so I turned and saw Ashton staring at me with a weird look on his face. Shooting him a smile, I pulled my hand from under the water and made my way back to him. Terry brought us a few paper towels to dry our hands and arms. Thanking him, I dried my arm and hand before sliding my sleeve back down. Turning to Ashton, I saw he was waiting patiently for me. We silently made our way to the front of the building, seeing everything there.

When we got to the front of the aquarium, I felt

Ashton's big warm hand wrap around mine. Before I could even look up at him, I was being tugged toward the gift shop.

"Ashton, what are you doing?" I asked as he pulled me into the gift shop.

"Pick whatever you want." He dropped my hand. I couldn't help but feel cold once his hand left mine. For some reason, I felt like I was missing something the moment his hand disappeared.

"What?"

"Pick something." He gestured around the shop. He gave me a firm look when I opened my mouth to protest. I started looking around. As I turned around, something caught my eye. I quickly walked over to it and reached for it. It was a dolphin necklace that was a very pretty deep blue color. It wasn't that large, and it was just simple, but something about it was gorgeous. I softly ran my finger over it. It wasn't like it was real or fragile, but I couldn't help but want to be gentle with it.

"You like it?" Ashton said, not really sounding like he was asking a question. All I did was nod. Before I could blink, the necklace was pulled out of my hands and Ashton was pulling his phone out taking a picture of it.

"W-What are you doing?" I asked, watching him.

"I'm going to send a picture of this to a jewelry store and they can make a better one," he said simply. As soon as he finished his sentence, I ripped the necklace from his hand.

"No!"

"Why? I can get you a better version that isn't

cheap."

"That doesn't matter." He looked at me weird so I continued. "Even though it is cheap, it has better meaning than a replica. It doesn't matter about the price. When I'll look at this, I'll remember everything that happened today and not that you got it made so it wouldn't be 'so cheap. I want this one," I said firmly.

Ashton stared at me almost in amazement, but I shrugged that off. I was not going to let him spend a lot of money on a necklace so it could be better than this one. The whole reason everyone got something at the stupid gift shop was to remember everything that happened and the things they'd done while at that place. Everyone knew it was cheap shit and that it would turn green, as well as your skin, but that didn't matter. I stared him down, holding the necklace against me. Finally, he nodded and reached for the necklace. Letting him take it, I followed him to the cashier. The lady rang it up and it came to fifteen dollars. Kind of expensive for a necklace, but it was New York after all. She handed it to me and gave me a smile.

"Here you go, sweetie. You're lucky to have a man like him," she said, looking at Ashton. I could feel my cheeks heating up, and avoided Ashton's gaze on me.

"She is lucky to have me." He smirked at me. I just rolled my eyes and thanked the lady before leaving the gift shop. I heard Ashton's footsteps behind me. I pushed open the doors and the chilly air hit me in the face. "Thank you," Ashton said in a high-pitched voice. He responded to himself with

"You're welcome" in his regular voice. I couldn't help but laugh softly at him.

"Thank you for the necklace," I said as his limo came to a stop in front of us. "I love it."

"You're welcome." He opened the car door for me. Nodding in thanks, I slid inside and a minute later, Ashton was next to me. As the car started forward, my thoughts went back to everything that happened today. I went on a date with a hot billionaire today. Me! Ordinary, boring, weird, ugly me! I couldn't wait to freak out when I got home later. I could honestly say today was one of the best days I'd ever had. The car ride back to my house was quiet but not uncomfortable. I could feel the warmth radiating off Ashton's body next to me. I could smell his cologne. I couldn't tell you what he smelled like, but whatever it was smelled amazing. I could literally smell him all day long.

Before I knew it, the limo came to a stop in front of my apartment. I was surprised that we got here so quick. Ashton was already outside waiting for me by the time I had said goodbye and thank you to Clark. Stepping out of the car, I turned to Ashton.

"I'll walk you up," he said.

"No, no, that's okay. I don't want you to leave your car running," I started to say but was cut off by one of his fingers pressed against my lips.

"I'm walking you up," he said sternly. I nodded against his finger and let him pull me into my building. We silently rode the elevator to the fifth level and got out. We came to a stop in front of my door, and I didn't know if I should kiss him or just say thank you and bye. Before I could decide, I saw him move down and felt his warm lips press against mine. This was our second kiss and I had to say it was toe-curling. His lips were firm and soft against mine as he softly moved them. I kissed him back but before it could go any further, he pulled back. I knew my face was flushed and my lips were slightly swollen.

"T-thank you for today," I breathed out as I looked up at him.

"You are welcome. I better go. See you later." He pressed one last kiss to my lips. He sent me a smirk then walked off. I watched him leave, trying hard to not to stare at his butt. The moment he disappeared out of sight, I put my key in the door and walked in closing it behind me. I leaned against the closed door and stared up at the ceiling. I couldn't stop the huge grin that spread across my face and a hand from reaching up to touch my kissed lips. I knew that in the future, if Ashton kept doing what he was doing, I knew my heart wouldn't be the same after.

Chapter 10

Layla

Thankfully, Kacey wasn't home, so I was able to relax for a little while before being interrogated about my date with Ashton. After leaning against the door, I set my stuff down and plopped down on my couch. Everything that happened over our "date" ran through my mind, putting a smile on my face. I sat there in my clothes just staring at the blank TV, trying not to reach for my phone and see if Ashton has already texted me. Stupid, I know, but I couldn't seem to get rid of Ashton. Before I could check my phone again, Kacey burst through the door.

"Tell me everything!" she demanded after she set her purse down on the table by the door and jumped on the couch next to me. Sighing, I dove into the storytelling Kacey everything from the moment we left to the kiss when he dropped me back off. Kacey sat there in silence just staring at me.

"Whoa," was all she said as she absorbed

everything I had told her. "Sounds like a pretty awesome date. Who would have known that Ashton Miller would spend the day with you at an aquarium?"

"Geez, thanks for that," I said, playing with my new necklace.

"You're welcome. Anyways, did you guys say when you're going out again?"

"No, he didn't say anything. He just said, 'I'll see you later' and that was it." I tried hard not to sound too sad about that.

"Don't worry, he will ask you out again. He has to." She got up. "What do you want for dinner?" I glanced at the clock above the TV and saw it was six already. *Wow, I was out with Ashton all day.*

"I don't care. Want to make something or order out?" I asked, getting up and stretching.

"Order out. Chinese sound good to you?" Kacey yelled from in the kitchen.

"Yeah, sounds good. Want me to order it?" Hearing a vague yes, I grabbed my phone and dialed the Chinese restaurant from down the street. Kacey and I have ordered take-out from there so many times I have the number memorized by now. Shung Ho had the best Pad Thai and orange chicken ever. After I ordered our usual, I went to my bedroom to change into my comfy sweats and a big t-shirt.

I was the kind of girl who, immediately after getting home, would change into PJs or sweats. I don't see how people can just sit around in their regular clothes all day. I don't find it comfortable but of course, that's just me. After I changed and went to wash my face, I heard the doorbell ring. That was fast but with the place being practically next door, it doesn't take long, and the Chinese family that owns the restaurant knows Kacey and me. Before I could leave my room and go pay, Kacey was already there thanking the guy while handing him the money. After she shut the door, I walked out and toward her.

"Kacey, I was going to pay tonight," I said.

"No, it's fine, Lay. I got it." Knowing she won't budge, I just rolled my eyes and walked over to the couch pulling my hair up in the process. Kacey spread the containers on our coffee table and went to grab forks and napkins. I opened the four containers and almost started drooling. I didn't realize how hungry I was until seeing Pad Thai, orange chicken, teriyaki chicken, and fried rice. As soon as Kacey came back with forks and napkins, I grabbed the remote and turned on the TV. Turning it to our favorite show, *Friends,* we dug into our food.

We ate in silence as watched. After eating all the food in under thirty minutes, we started cleaning up.

"So...are you going to text him?" Kacey asked suddenly as we finished cleaning up.

"I don't know. Maybe tomorrow," I said, wiping my hands.

"Why tomorrow? Text him now."

"No, I don't want to seem too eager."

Silence wrapped around us. I turned to Kacey to see why she was silent and just as I turned, I saw her lunge for my phone that was sitting on the couch. Just as quick as she went for it, I was behind her.

"Kay, no, don't!" I yelled, falling onto the couch a little bit away from Kacey.

"No, you need to talk to him!" she yelled back at me, reaching for my phone that was just in front of her.

"No, I don't!" I reached for her and grabbed her ankle, trying to stop her. As I pulled her back, her arm reached out and snatched my phone. "Kay, don't you dare!"

"It's for your own good!" I gripped her leg tighter, pulling her toward me. Just as I thought, I stopped her from texting Ashton by pulling her right to me but then I heard her yell "'Yes! It's done!'" I let her leg go and stared at her.

"You did not just text him!"

"Yes, I did. And you are welcome." She stood up and dropped my phone by me as she walked off.

"Kacey!" I yelled after her, but she didn't answer or turn around. *Great, just great.* I stared down at my phone waiting for Ashton's text to come through. I finally stood up. *Wait, why am I waiting for his reply? Get a grip, Layla, you don't have to wait around for him. Get up and do something and leave your phone alone.* Nodding to myself, I left my phone on the couch and headed to find Kacey. Finding her in the kitchen leaning against the counter on her phone, I sighed and walked over to her. She looked up from her phone and sent me a sheepish smile.

"You're not really mad at me, are you?" she asked, giving me her puppy dog eyes.

"No, I'm not," I said, shaking my head and

leaning beside her against the counter.

"Okay, good. I did it for you because I know you would never do it. I don't know how much I could have taken you checking your phone every five seconds."

"I wasn't checking it every five seconds!" I defended myself even though I knew she was right. Ever since I got home I'd been checking my phone to see if Ashton had texted me, or if I had missed a call or text.

"Yes, you were. Lay, I just want you to be happy. You've never been happy. Or, at least not since you moved away from your parents." She's right. The moment I was free from my parents was a day I will never forget. It was the day Kacey and I left for NYU and I never looked back. For most families going off to college is a sad, depressing thing, but for me, I couldn't be happier leaving and not ever coming back.

"I know, Kacey, but I don't want to start to think he likes me when he doesn't or even won't. I'm not going to let my heart get broken by some hot millionaire bachelor."

"I see what you mean and I won't let him hurt you, or I will hurt where the sun don't shine. But see where it goes before writing it off because you never know where it will lead." I nodded knowing that she was right.

"When did you get so smart?" I asked her. "I used to be the smart one," I said jokingly.

"Whatever, I've always been smarter than you." She rolled her eyes at me.

"Nuh uh, I've always been the smarty pants

here."

"Says the girl who just said 'smarty pants.'"

"Yeah, I'll have you know that word is in the dictionary."

"And how do you know that? You just sit in your room and read the dictionary for fun?"

I narrowed my eyes at her. "You're lucky you're my best friend and that I'm tired from tackling you on the couch." Kacey opened her mouth to reply, but the ringing of my phone interrupted her. We both looked at each other wide-eyed. A second later, we both shot toward the living room. I wanted to get there before Kacey because, knowing her, she would answer and tell him something I didn't want her to. Kacey was ahead of me, so I did the only thing that came to my mind: I pushed her…hard. As Kay flopped down onto the other side of the couch, I jumped to my phone and quickly answered it.

"Hello," I answered breathlessly not having looked at the caller ID.

"Hello, Layla? Are you okay?" Ashton asked through the phone.

"What? Oh no, I'm fine just doing some…exercising," I answered, shooting a glare over at Kacey who was glaring right back at me for shoving her on the couch. I heard him chuckle through the phone.

"Anyways, I'm picking you up tomorrow around nine a.m. so be ready." The way he spoke was like a command. Just as I opened my mouth to say yes, the stupid voice in the back of my head had to remind me I worked tomorrow morning.

"Sorry, I can't…I have to work at seven," I said,

trying to hide my sadness. For only being with the guy for one day, I was already missing his presence.

"Just quit."

"Ashton, I just can't quit. It's my only job." I shook my head even though he couldn't see me.

"It's okay. I will just find you another job. I don't want you working at that place anymore."

"No, Ashton, I can't. I worked hard to get my job there and I am fine staying. It is not a bad place to work."

"Layla, you wear booty shorts and a tight shirt. I don't want you there," he said, his voice becoming hard. This man already thinks he can tell me what to do. I am not letting that happen.

"It is fine," I said, even though I knew he was right. It was weird wearing such revealing clothes at such a fancy restaurant, and I didn't like showing my ass off to strangers but it was the only place I could get a job that pays enough for my side of the rent. "Sorry, Ashton, but I can't go tomorrow…and I have to go to bed. It's late. Thank you for a good day and good night." I quickly ended the call and set my phone down in my lap. *Did I just hang up on Ashton Miller? I'm in deep shit now.*

"Layla, what just happened?" Kacey asked, bringing me back out of my thoughts.

"I may have just hung up on Ashton." I stared at my phone in my lap.

"What was he asking that made you hang up on him?" she wondered.

"He wanted to take me out tomorrow but I have work. So, I told him I couldn't then he went on about how he doesn't want me working at the restaurant anymore and that I should quit." I turned toward her. "Kay, I can't just quit my job. It's the only one I have and it pays the rent."

"Lay," Kacey said, shaking her head. "He is right, you know. That place is all the way across town, you have to wear a ridiculous outfit even though it's considered 'fancy,' and no one ever tips you. Maybe Ashton is right and you should quit and look for another job."

The idea of quitting sounded appealing, but I'm not the kind of person who just gives up. I hate my job, yes, but I just can't quit when I have nothing else to fall on. Kacey must have read my face because she put her hand on my arm.

"Just think about it, okay? You don't have to make a decision yet." I nodded at her and shot her a small smile. I knew that the conversation had turned one hundred eighty degrees, so Kacey broke our tense silence. "Now about you shoving me on the couch." She glared at me.

***

Ashton

Everything that had happened today was better than I had anticipated. I found myself enjoying Layla's company and loved talking to her. She wasn't like my other hook-ups. She was smart, quiet, reserved, shy, and funny. After I had dropped her off at her apartment, I couldn't stop replaying kissing her in my mind. Her lips were so soft and warm. I would have kissed her forever, but I had found myself pulling away from her. The way she looked up at me with hooded eyes and swollen lips almost made me claim her lips one more time, but I knew if I did that I wouldn't stop until I had ravished her completely, making her mine.

Whoa. Where did those thoughts come from? I wondered to myself as my driver drove me home. I just barely met the girl. I could not be thinking about making her mine only. Shaking my head at my thoughts, I tried to think of something else. The harder I tried to not think of Layla, the more I did. There was something about her that was addicting to me. Maybe it was her stubbornness, or that look in her eyes that shown sadness and pain, or even the way she talked back at me like no one had in a long time.

Thanking Clark and sending him home for the night, I walked into my penthouse suit making my way to my bedroom unbuttoning my shirt along the way. After changing into some more comfortable attire, I walked toward my kitchen. Even though I am a millionaire, I like to do my own cooking. When I bought this hotel/suite, I made sure the kitchen was exactly how I wanted it. Most say it's weird for a guy to like cooking, but for me it reminds me of when my mom would ask me to help her cook dinner, teaching me everything she knew. Ever since I was eight years old, I helped my mom cook meals and when I could, I made my own as well. Everyone had to have their favorite hobby, and mine was cooking.

I took everything out that I needed to make myself a grilled cheese, which was something I made when I didn't want to cook something big for just myself. While waiting for the pan to warm up, I got the bread out and buttered both sides lightly and got to cutting pieces of cheese. About ten minutes later, I had myself two grill cheese sandwiches. I walked to my office and sat down, doing some stuff that needed to be done for tomorrow at work.

Just because I'm the CEO of my family's business does not mean I don't do any work. Anything that goes on I know about, and I fix it. My company, Miller Enterprises, was well known for having great workers, and great outcomes to whatever we do. The company was passed down to me by my father, John Miller, when he stepped down at the age of fifty-five due to health issues. My father built our company, plus all the others that have expanded over the country, from the bottom up.

All through high school and college, I knew I was expected to take over the company whenever my dad decided to step down, but at the time I actually wanted to do something different. Like be a chef or a fireman instead of a business man, but with all the pressure from my father and his partners, I graduated college with a business degree and immediately started working under my father getting trained to take over. Now, three years later, here I am doing just that. My sister got out of having to follow our father, but instead had to follow our mother.

My mother, Claire Miller, is one of the highest paid lawyers here in New York. She came from a small poor family and grew up on the outskirts of the city. After working hard all through high school, my mom got a full-ride scholarship to Harvard to become a lawyer. Determined to make something of her life, she worked hard and became a great attorney. My mother was not a workaholic though. Growing up, she was there when we needed her and if she had to choose her children over work, she would. Now, at the age of fifty-two, she was thinking of retiring and letting my sister take over her job.

My sister, Ariel Miller, followed in my mom's footsteps and worked hard all through high school and college, and was now a pretty successful lawyer at the age of twenty-three. She was the youngest to make partner at her firm, where my mother also works from time to time. My sister is the best. She is one of my best friends and is always annoying me, but I love her.

Suddenly, the ring of my phone jerked me out of my thoughts and work. Grabbing my phone, I saw it was from Layla.

To: Ashton
From: Layla
Hey. What are you up to?

I couldn't stop the smile from forming on my face. Layla already missed me. I stared at the phone for a few minutes trying to decide what to text back. An idea popped into my head. I should take Layla out again tomorrow. But this time I'll take her to the zoo or something, maybe let her decide. Just the thought of seeing Layla again tomorrow made me grin wider. *Wow, I'm starting to act like a girl.* Shaking my head at myself, I picked up my phone and called her.

"Hello," Layla answered, sounding breathless. *What is she doing?* I wondered.

"Hello, Layla? Are you okay?" I asked.

"What? Oh no, I'm fine, just doing some…exercising," she said, her breathing turning back to normal. I chuckled and shook my head.

"Anyways, I'm picking you up tomorrow around nine a.m. so be ready."

"Sorry, I can't…I have to work at seven." I could hear regret or sadness in her voice.

"Just quit." For some reason, just the thought of her in those booty shorts and that tight shirt made me clench my jaw. I could just imagine men's eyes on her body.

"Ashton, I can't just quit. It's my only job."

"It's okay. I will just find you another job. I don't want you working at that place anymore."

"No, Ashton, I can't. I worked hard to get my job there and I am fine staying. It is not a bad place to work." Her voice was firm.

"Layla, you wear booty shorts and a tight shirt. I don't want you there," I said, getting irritated. I was not going to budge on this.

"It is fine." There was a pause. "Sorry, Ashton, but I can't go tomorrow…and I have to go to bed. It's late. Thank you for a good day and good night." She hung up. I stared down at my phone with a raised eyebrow. Layla just hung up on me, but for some reason, I wasn't mad at her. I was just amused.

Layla Kingston, you don't know what you got yourself into. When I want something, I will get it.

Chapter 11

Layla

"Miss, excuse me!" a voice yelled two tables down from where I currently was. Sighing under my breath, I turned and shot a smile at the customer.

"Yes? How can I help you?" I asked, acting polite when all I wanted to do was yell. It was eleven o'clock and I was ready to go home.

"I ordered medium rare for my steak and it is well done." The man held up his plate and stared at it like it was a live octopus or something. *He wasn't even my table,* I thought bitterly.

"Oh, I am sorry, sir. I will go and get you another steak properly made," I said, grabbing the plate.

"Yes, you will and I will not be paying for it either," the man said rather rudely. I just nodded while biting my tongue. I walked to the kitchen and asked the cook to make me another steak and made sure it was rare. Five minutes later the bell rang and I grabbed the steak. After dropping it back off at the rude man's table, I made my rounds again seeing if anyone needed anything. Just when I thought I had a few minutes of freedom, Kayleen, the hostess, called my name.

"Layla, I hate to do this to you but Kim can't come in today. I need you to take her shift," Kayleen said, her eyes pleading for me to say yes.

"What's her shift?" I asked, sighing.

"Eleven to four." I inwardly groaned. Great, just great.

"Yeah, fine, I will," I said even though I knew I would regret it.

"Thank you, Layla, you are the best! Her tables are two, four, six, fourteen, and seventeen today." Nodding at her, I wrote them down my little notepad and got back to work.

Four hours had passed and I was so ready to go home. My feet hurt and my head was pounding. Taking a deep breath, I picked up my tray full of food and left the kitchen, heading to my table. Just as I set the food down and was heading back, I felt a big hand grab my ass. Whirling around, I saw a man at one of the tables smirking at me. I narrowed my eyes at him. He wasn't too bad looking with dark brown hair, brown eyes, and a strong jawline, but there was something about his smile that wasn't right.

"Excuse me," I bit out and turned back around. Inside, I was fuming.

"Little lady, where are you going?" the man called out. I ignored him and kept walking. I didn't get too far until a hand wrapped around my wrist. The man spun me around and pulled me right up against him. "You can't walk away from me, pretty little lady."

"Let me go," I hissed, feeling people starting to stare at us. I didn't want to cause a scene, so I tried pulling away from him but he had a good grip on me.

"You can't go walking around in those sexy little shorts and not expect someone to notice." These kinds of moments really made me hate my job. I felt like I was a stripper at some club instead of at an expensive restaurant. With the guy's hold on me tightening, I could feel myself starting to panic. I did the only thing that came to my mind even though I knew I would get in trouble for it. I brought my knee up and kneed the man in the groin. His hold instantly loosened as he fell to the ground holding his junk. I took a step back feeling myself shaking slightly.

"Don't ever touch me!" I hissed loudly at the guy. As I opened my mouth to say something else, a loud voice boomed over everyone's sudden chatter. I gulped and turned around seeing my boss, Joseph, standing there and glaring at me. *Shit,* I thought. When my boss jerked his head, I knew he wanted me to follow him to his office. Putting my head down, I weaved my way through the tables and to his office. Out of all the days to be here, Joseph had to come in. He held the door open for me and I slid inside and took a seat in a chair.

"Ms. Kingston, or can I call you Layla?" Joseph asked, sitting down across from me behind his desk.

"Layla is fine," I almost stuttered out.

"Layla, what you did back there was

unprofessional. We do not hurt our customers." I opened my mouth to protest but he lifted his hand to stop me. "I don't care what he did; you should not have kneed him. Now one of two things can happen right now," he said, looking straight at me. I watched as his eyes traveled down from my face to my chest, and if the desk weren't there, they'd probably go even lower. He flicked his eyes back up to my face and leaned back in his chair.

"You need this job pretty bad, don't you?" He intertwined his hands in front of him.

"Y-yes sir," I stuttered out.

"Well, in order for me to let you stay here after hurting a special customer, I'm going to need you to do something." The longer he stared at me, the more uncomfortable I felt. Something didn't feel right about this. "You see...I am a lonely man and every once in a while, I need someone to take care of me." He drew out the word "care." I instantly knew where this was going from the hungry look in his eyes.

"Are you asking me to sleep with you?" I asked, curling my hands into fists in my lap. This man really wanted me to sleep with him to keep my job?

"I wouldn't say it that way; it's more of an agreement to help one another out." The way he said it was like he was proposing a deal to a big investor. Suddenly, a wave of anger washed over me. I quickly stood up, feeling my face turning red with anger.

"Listen to me, Joseph." I spit out his name "I will not sleep with you to save my job. I don't need it that bad. I am done with this place. I don't need some disgusting, fat, old, perv trying to make me sleep with him just because I was defending myself from being touched. I quit!" I yelled at him. Turning on my heel, I stormed out of his office and toward the workers' lockers to grab my stuff.

My body was shaking from how angry I was. Ripping open my locker, I grabbed my bag and slammed it shut. Too mad to say goodbye to my friends here, I walked out the door glad to be done with this place. The further I walked, the more my eyes started to water and before I knew it, I had tears rolling down my cheeks. With shaky hands, I reached for my phone. For some reason, I called the person I least expected to call. I tried to stop my crying as my phone rung but they wouldn't stop.

"Hello?" answered a familiar deep voice.

"A-Ashton...I need you."

***

Ashton

I got up the next morning and headed to work slightly later than normal. The whole ride there I kept thinking of Layla and what I was going to do when I saw her next. I was seriously tempted to drop by her work today and talk to her, but I knew that would just piss her off even more by doing that. *Since when have you cared about other people besides yourself?* Ignoring my thoughts, I walked onto the level where my office was.

"Good morning, Mr. Miller," a feminine voice said to my right. Standing next to me was a small blonde woman who I think worked in marketing, but I had no idea.

"Good morning," I greeted her. She was wearing a very tight pencil shirt and an almost see-through white blouse with a bright pink bra underneath. Her face was caked in makeup, making her look like a stripper or something. Normally I would flirt and sleep with her before ignoring her, but ever since I met Layla I couldn't look at another woman without comparing them to Layla, and none seemed to match up. Walking past her, I headed to my office.

"Morning, Judy," I said, smiling at my receptionist. Judy had been my receptionist since I came on board with the company. She was in her late fifties and had a few strands of gray in her hair. She was almost like a mother to me, making sure I was on time for everything and always keeping me in line.

"Good morning, Ashton." She was also the only person I let call me Ashton at the office. "How are you?"

"I am doing good. How are you? How is Bill?" I asked. Bill was her husband and they had been married for forty years. They met in high school and married soon after graduating.

"I am good, as is Bill." She smiled up at me. "Oh, you have a board meeting in fifteen minutes."

"Okay, thank you, Judy." I smiled back and headed inside my office. My office was pretty big and had an incredible view of downtown New York. The view was even better at nighttime when the whole city was lit up.

The day flew by pretty fast and soon enough, it

was three o'clock. I had meetings all day and each one was something different. I finally sat down at my desk and rubbed my forehead. I could feel a headache forming. I looked down and checked my phone wondering why I hadn't heard from Layla today. All day I kept glancing at my phone, making sure I didn't miss anything from her. *Maybe she is really mad at me.* Just as I picked up my phone to send her a text, my phone started buzzing in my hand. Seeing Layla's name pop up, I answered it.

"Hello?" I answered. I heard sniffling through the phone and immediately straightened up.

"A-Ashton...I need you," Layla whispered. Instantly I was up and out of my chair, grabbing my suit jacket.

"Baby, where are you?" I asked, not liking the sound of her crying.

"Outside of w-work."

"I'm on my way." I hung up and left my office. "Judy, I need you to cancel anything else for the rest of the day," I said over my shoulder as I walked to the elevator. After I pressed the button multiple times, the doors finally opened. Not giving a chance for anyone else to get on, I pressed the close button and waited as it carried me down to the lobby. On the way down, I called Clark and told him to meet me downstairs in two minutes. Once the doors were open, I walked briskly to the front doors and saw Clark waiting there. Sliding inside of the car, I practically shouted at him.

"To The River Cafe and hurry." Clark nodded and drove to Layla's work. I ignored the annoying voice in my head telling me I was stupid for rushing for to see if Layla was okay. Before I knew it, Clark came to a stop in front of The River Cafe. I jumped out and looked around trying to find Layla. I turned to my right and saw a little bit ahead of me was a hunched-over figure. It moved and I saw a flash of brown hair. Next thing I knew, my legs were carrying me over to Layla quickly.

"Layla," I shouted as I drew nearer. Just as I was a foot away from her, she ran over to me and practically jumped into my arms. Her arms wrapped around my neck as mine went to her waist. I felt her body shaking as she started crying, making my neck wet. "Shhhh." I rubbed her back. I have never in my life comforted a crying woman, but with Layla, it seemed to come easy to me. "It's okay, love."

As we stood there for a little while, I felt her tears coming to a stop. With her arms still wrapped around my neck, I swung her up into my arms and carried her bridal style to the car. Clark stepped out and opened the door for me. It was awkward getting into the car with her in my arms, but I made do. Laying her in my lap, I mouthed to Clark to take us to my apartment. When I gently rubbed her back, I felt her body relax. As we crossed the bridge into downtown, we hit traffic but that was okay with me. The longer Layla was in my lap the more I felt complete, a foreign feeling to me. I looked down at her and saw she was asleep. Seeing her looking so peaceful pulled at my heart strings. She looked so innocent and delicate as she lay in my arms. Her cheeks were stained with tears and her hair looked like she had pulled it, but to me, she looked even more beautiful.

I moved away a loose strand of hair that fell from her ponytail. *What happened to make her cry?* I wondered. *Whatever or whomever it was, I will make sure they pay. No one will ever make Layla cry.* The longer I looked down at her, the more I became certain that I would not let any harm come to Layla.

Chapter 12

Layla

The hand came down and smacked hard against my cheek. My head snapped back and I could feel my cheek swelling and burning. Tears brimmed my eyes but I held them in; I couldn't let them see me cry or they would do it twice as hard.

"You are such a waste of space. I don't know why your mother and I even had you!" my father said as he stood beside me. Before I could even look up, his fist connected to my stomach and I slumped over, all the breath in my body escaping me. I fell to my knees trying to gulp in some air as my father stood over me with a cruel smile across his face. I knew my cheek would be bruised in the morning, and that I would have a pretty good-sized bruise on my stomach. Although the pain was nothing new to me, I never got used to it.

"I think it's time you learn what your place really is." I saw his feet move away from me. Instead of relaxing, I tensed up even more as what

114

he said ran through my mind. A deep, wrenching feeling wedged itself in my stomach as my mind came up with what he would do. I heard his feet shuffling back to me and my eyes shot up. I bit back a scream as my father held a big cooking knife in his hand. As he advanced on me, I couldn't stop myself from moving backward, away from him. He really has lost his mind this time, *I thought. Just as he stood a foot away from me, I opened my mouth and let out a scream.*

I jolted awake as I felt arms shaking me. My eyes snapped open and I moved back on the bed.

"No, no don't hurt me!" I yelled as I kept backing up until my back hit something. Turning my head, I saw it was a headboard. I felt the bed dip and I felt my heart speed up.

"Layla, it's okay. It's just me," a familiar soothing voice said. Upon hearing Ashton's voice, my heart seemed to calm down. I couldn't stop myself from going over to Ashton and wrapping my arms around him. His cologne surrounded me, and I breathed its scent in deeply. "It's okay," he said as he rubbed my back in circles.

I hadn't had that dream in almost four months. *Why now?* I thought as I calmed down. I lay still in Ashton's arms, not wanting to move in case it ruined the perfect moment.

"Are you okay?" Ashton asked as he still rubbed my back. I nodded into his chest, starting to feel embarrassed. "Do you want to tell me what happened today?" I knew I had to explain what happened to Ashton, but I knew telling him would wreck the peacefulness around us. I eventually sighed and pulled out of his embrace. My body seemed to go cold as soon as his arms fell from me and I had to stop myself from launching back into his arms.

"Well...I went to work today and everything was fine, even after I had to take someone else's shift. It was getting close to the end of my shift when a guy smacked my ass. It's not like it hasn't happened before, but this guy got up and kept coming onto me so I did the only thing that came to mind; I kick him in his...private area," I explained, staring down at my hands. "My boss saw and told me to follow him to talk. Well, long story short, he wanted me to do something in order to keep my job and I said no and quit. Then I called you." I waited for Ashton to say something but he stayed silent. *Maybe I shouldn't have told him. Does he think that's a terrible excuse to quit?*

After about five minutes of silence, I looked up not being able to handle him not saying anything. Surprised, I saw him sitting there with his hands in fists and his jaw clenched almost painfully.

"Ashton?" I asked, slightly scared. "Ashton?"

"Did he touch you?" he finally bit out, his voice hard and tight.

"What? No." That seemed to calm him down slightly, but not much. "Ashton, what's wrong?"

"I will destroy that man."

"Stop. Ashton, it's fine. Nothing happened to me. Plus, I quit and isn't that what you wanted?"

"I don't care if you're fine or not! That man has no right to ask or treat you that way. And yes, you are never going back to that place," Ashton said. I wanted to argue with him but I knew that he wouldn't budge and it would only make things worse, so instead, I stayed silent waiting for him to cool off. My stomach took the opportunity to make mating calls. My cheeks flared as Ashton looked down at me in amusement.

"Hungry?" he asked, a small smile on his face. Seeing him smile made him instantly one hundred times hotter. His blue eyes brightened up. I nodded, not able to find my voice. "Let's go make something." He got off the bed and held his hand out for me, and I instantly grabbed it and let him pull me off the bed. He kept his hand in mine as we made our way to his kitchen. Walking through the door, I was once again hit with awe at his beautiful kitchen. "What would you like?" His voice interrupted my gawking.

"Um, how about spaghetti?" I asked, hoping it wouldn't be too much trouble. For some odd reason, it sounded good to me at the moment.

"Fine with me," he said as he started to move around the kitchen gracefully. By looking at him and seeing him grabbing what he needed, I knew he was familiar with a kitchen. For some reason, that surprised me. I never would have pictured Ashton Miller as a cook in a million years. Again, it made him even hotter. I felt awkward just standing there and staring at him.

"Need any help?" I asked, hoping he would say yes.

"Sure. Here is the pan; can you fill it up with water?" He handed me a pan. Smiling, I took it and started filling it up. As I did my thing, Ashton was opening cans of tomato sauce and pouring it into another pan.

"Are you making homemade spaghetti sauce?" I asked, bringing the almost-full pan to the stove and setting it down.

"Yes. I think it's better than a can."

"Me too. Where are the spaghetti noodles?"

"Over there, top shelf," he said, gesturing to a cabinet with his head.

Opening it up, I saw the noodles and reached up to grab them but found I couldn't reach. I tried again and then tried hopping, but my fingers barely made it. Suddenly, I felt a warm body pressed against my back and an arm reaching past mine to grab a package of noodles. I felt Ashton's strong chest pressed against my back and felt my knees go weak. "Here you go," he whispered in my ear, his voice low and husky.

He stepped away from me and I let out a breath I didn't know I was holding. I was breathing slightly heavy and my knees felt weak as I walked over to my pan and set the package down. Something about Ashton made me want to jump him then and there. After cooling off some, I turned around to see him stirring something and moving his head to an unknown beat. Smiling, I slid up behind him and stood on my tippy toes to see over his shoulder.

"What are you doing?" I asked into his ear. He jumped slightly but then pretended like he didn't.

"Mixing. Care to help?"

"Sure. What do you need?" I walked to his side and saw a bunch of spices sitting around his bowl.

"Can you start putting some spices in here while I stir it?" Nodding, I reached for the garlic first and started sprinkling it in. I never really measured stuff like this and it seemed Ashton didn't either because he didn't say anything about it. We did that in comfortable silence. After stirring in the spices I put in, Ashton lifted the spoon to me. "Taste it," he said. Smiling, I leaned toward the spoon but instead of licking the spoon, I put some on my finger and tasted it. It needed something, so I grabbed more stuff and put it in then tasted it again.

"Good," I said, looking up at Ashton.

"Good," he repeated after me and went and put the pot on the stove, warming it up. Following his lead, I turned on the burner to start the noodles. While waiting, I leaned against the side of the counter and looked at Ashton. He was still in his work clothes but had his suit jacket off, and his gray button-up shirt sleeves were rolled up to his elbows showing his strong forearms. He had a slight stubble gracing his cheeks, and his brown hair was messy like he had run his fingers through it multiple times.

If you had to ask me why I called Ashton instead of Kacey, I couldn't tell you. Even though I had just met him, I felt like I knew him and could trust him. I knew I should be hesitant to do so because I didn't know what his true intentions were. Everything inside of me screamed that I should run away as far as I could before I get hurt, but I couldn't make myself. The longer I stared at him, the more I felt insignificant. I felt so plain and poor against Ashton. He was so handsome and could have any girl he wanted, I couldn't wrap my head around why he would be wasting his time on someone like me. Someone so boring and broken.

"Layla?" Ashton said, breaking me out of my self-drowning thoughts.

"Hmmm." I shook my head and looked at him.

"Ready to eat?" He didn't bring up that I zoned out and I was glad. I didn't want to explain how I was thinking about how hot he was and how I wasn't.

"Yes, please." I nodded and took the plate he offered to me. At the mention of food, my stomach seemed to awaken and was making gurgling noises. I blushed as Ashton chuckled but he silently spooned a handful of noodles on my plate, as well as sauce. It looked like a lot, but I knew I would be eating it all. I stood off to the side waiting for Ashton, not knowing if he wanted us to eat somewhere besides at the bar.

"We'll just eat here at the bar since it is only the two of us." He seemed to read my mind. As I walked to a seat, Ashton grabbed up napkins and silverware.

"Sorry, I would have grabbed some," I said apologetically as I slipped onto a stool.

"No, you're fine." He set down a napkin and fork for me and put his stuff down beside me. "Would you care for a drink?"

"Sure."

"I have beer, wine, water, or juice if you'd like." Deciding that beer didn't really go with our meal, I opted for the wine. He shot me a smile as he grabbed an already open bottle from the fridge and two glasses. Once he was seated beside me, he poured us some.

"Cheers," he said, his blue eyes piercing my gray ones.

"Cheers." Our glasses clinked and we both took a sip, our eyes not wavering from each other's. We both turned to our food and dug in. Even though there was nothing special with the spaghetti, it tasted amazing. Maybe it was because I was so hungry and hadn't eaten all day or that Ashton made it, but either way, I had to stop a moan from escaping my lips as I ate.

We were silent as we ate but it wasn't an awkward silence. It seemed we were both so comfortable with each other that we didn't need to fill the air with constant chatter. Every time Ashton would move, I would catch a drift of his cologne. I didn't know what he used, but whatever it was it became my new favorite scent.

"So, what are you going to do now that you don't have a job?" Ashton asked. I found myself closer to him than I should be and moved back. I took a sip of my wine before I answered, hoping to win some composure back after practically smelling him.

"I don't know. I guess I better start job hunting tomorrow," I said and frowned at the thought. I've always hated job hunting and interviews. I was never really good at them and usually messed them up so that I wouldn't get a call back. I was actually surprised when I got a call saying I was hired at the River Cafe.

"Well...are you good at making phone calls?"

Ashton asked suddenly.

"I-I guess," I answered, caught off-guard.

"How about running errands for someone, keeping track of schedules, following orders?" The last one sounded very kinky to me, but I quickly got my mind out of the gutter. I nodded, still confused. Ashton leaned back in his chair and rubbed his hand across his jaw.

"Well, it seems that I have an opening at my company. Would that be of interest to you at all?" I sat there in shock. *Was he offering me a job?*

"I, uh." I cleared my throat and continued when I found my voice. "Yes, that would be great!" I practically shouted at him. I jumped out of my chair and wrapped my arms around his neck. "Ashton, that would be amazing." Working at a company that large and well known would be amazing, even if it were some low-level job like being a receptionist. When Kacey and I were looking Ashton up, we read about his company and I knew he paid his employees very well and everyone wanted a job there as well.

"But you haven't even heard what the position is," Ashton said in my ear as I tightly gripped him. Realizing he was right, I pulled away embarrassed at myself for jumping to conclusions.

"Sorry." I got back in my seat and calmed down.

"I am looking for an assistant who will be able to handle all my appointments, take care of my schedules, do paperwork, come to meetings with me. They will practically be with me every day and night. This person will have to know my company almost inside and out. Do you think you could do that?" he asked, his voice serious.

I sat there and thought about it. I actually knew I would say yes the moment he mentioned having to be with him every day and night. Other than being able to spend almost every waking moment with him, could I do the job? I think I could. I was very efficient and when I set my mind to something, I would do it whether it takes me forever or not. I knew it would be a lot of work and would be quite hard at times, but I also knew I couldn't let this opportunity pass me by either. Plus, whenever I get another job, this would look very good on my resume. I made my decision then and there.

"Yes, I can," I said confidently, or at least I tried to sound that way. Ashton stared long and hard at me, almost making me squirm in my seat. Finally, he nodded.

"Good. You start tomorrow."

"Tomorrow?" *So soon?*

"Yes. I want you there at six a.m. sharp." His voice was all business and I didn't even try to argue about how early that was. Looking up, I saw it was nine at night. *Oh god! Kacey's probably wondering where I am.* Seeing as the air had turned from fun and light to business, I slid off my stool.

"I guess I better get going then," I said, sending him a small smile. The feeling had changed drastically in just a short amount of time. Ashton just nodded and got up too.

"Oh wait, what about the dishes?" I said after I stood up.

"It's fine. I'll take care of them when I get back," Ashton said.

"I don't want to leave you with all these dishes," I shot back, looking at the pans and our dishes on the counter.

"Don't worry, I'll have my maid clean it up in the morning. Let's go. I'll drive you home." His hand pressed against my lower back. I finally caved as he led me to the front door.

As we reached the front door, I saw my bag hanging on a hook beside it. Knowing that Ashton put it there put a small smile on my face as I grabbed it and hung it over my shoulder. We walked in silence all the way down to the garage level and to his car. I tried not to stare in awe at his black 911 Carrera Porsche. I knew just a little bit about of cars to know this was a very nice car and super expensive. Being a gentleman, he opened the door for me, and I slid inside, gawking at the interior. The seats were black leather and it had a state-of-the-art stereo system. People were right; this car did scream luxury and sleekness. Ashton slid into the driver's seat and started the car. The engine purred to life and rumbled underneath me.

"Nice car," I commented as he backed out and exited the garage.

"Thank you, it's a 911—"

"Carrera Porsche," I finished.

"You know cars?" he asked, his voice full of surprise.

"Only a little. My ex-boyfriend was really into them so I picked up on a few things."

"Oh." The mention of an ex-boyfriend seemed to shut Ashton up as he drove me back to my apartment in silence. Instead of wondering what pissed him off, I stared at the window. *How did he change from happy to pissed off so fast?* I wondered. I've started to see he can change moods at the drop of a hat. Whether that's a good thing or not, I don't know. We pulled up to my apartment and I unbuckled myself. We walked inside and up to my door, and it was almost like deja vu as we stopped in the same spot as yesterday. It was hard to believe just yesterday I went on my first date with him and now here we are, after him picking me up and consoling me, to offering me a job. What a change in only one day.

"Well, thank you for everything today, Ashton. Thank you for picking me up, listening to me, making me dinner, and offering me a job. I don't know how I will ever be able to repay you," I said sincerely. I seemed to shake him out of his weird trance, and he turned to me with a soft expression.

"You're welcome, Layla. You can always call me if you need anything."

"Thank you. I guess I'll see you tomorrow bright and early," I said with a grin.

"Yes, you will. Good night, Layla," Ashton said as he leaned down and kissed the top of my forehead. Even though it wasn't on my lips, I could still feel my skin tingling. A lazy smile appeared on my face as he pulled away. "Good night." With that, he turned and walked away.

I turned and opened my door and slipped inside. All the lights were off in the house, so I quietly made my way to my room and set my stuff down. After plugging in my phone to charge, I quickly washed my face and changed out of my clothes and into PJs. Setting an alarm for 4:30 a.m., I slid under my covers. I quickly drifted off to sleep as I thought about Ashton and what would happen tomorrow.

Chapter 13

Layla

I woke up the next morning to the annoying sound of my alarm. I groaned and rolled over putting my pillow over my head. My alarm went quiet after a minute but then started right back up. Reaching blindly with my hand, I tried to slap the snooze button but my hand kept missing. I lifted my pillow up slightly and cracked open my eyes, staring at my alarm. Staring back at me was the time: 4:30 am. *Why the hell did I set an alarm for that early?* It took me a full good minute for yesterday's events to come back to mind and for me to wake up. I have work today! Faster than any normal person at 4:30 in the morning, I jumped out of bed and ran to my bathroom.

Starting the shower to get it warmed up, I stripped out of my PJs and quickly jumped in. Setting the alarm to 4:30 sounded insane but since Ashton wanted me there at 6 o'clock and it was my first day, I didn't want to be late. I took the quickest shower in history. Steam billowed around me as I dried off my body then headed back to my bedroom to get dressed. I knew this part would take me the longest because I had to find something an assistant to the big boss would wear and also be work appropriate, which turned out to be very difficult.

Fifteen minutes later I was standing there looking helplessly at my closet. Most of my clothes littered the ground and my closet looked like a war zone. *I have nothing to wear!* I thought hopelessly. Checking the clock, I saw it was five to five. Panic started to set in as I looked around my room trying to come up with something. An idea clicked in my head and I knew it was my only option. I had to go face my best friend/roommate at five in the morning. Saying a silent goodbye to myself, I made my way to Kacey's room. To say Kacey isn't a morning person is a big understatement. She doesn't believe in waking up any time before nine. Waking her up is like signing your own death warrant, which I was about to do.

Pushing her door open, I tried to be quiet as I walked to her bed. Taking a deep breath, I said her name and shook her shoulder. At this time of the morning, Kacey was usually dead to the world.

"Kacey," I said a little louder. When she didn't stir, I did the worst thing you could do in this situation. I went into her bathroom and filled a cup she had in there with cold water. Coming back to her bedside, I dipped a couple of fingers into the water and proceeded to flick the water at her face, Chinese water torture. Kacey's eyes burst open and stared at me.

"You!" Her voice was low from sleep, and dangerous. If her eyes had lasers in them, I would be burnt to a crisp by now. Maybe it was me, but her eyes seemed to glow red as she glared up at me. Uh oh, I woke the devil up! I backed away slowly.

"Kay, I am so sorry but I couldn't wake you. I need your help," I tried to say calmly, hoping it would help her not attack me.

"It is still dark outside," she seethed.

"I know, but I don't have anything to wear to work. I really need your help."

"Layla, you already have clothes for work." She groaned out, closing her eyes. She seemed to have calmed down slightly, which was good.

"Um, about that. I…don't work there anymore." Her eyes opened instantly.

"What?"

"I quit yesterday. I was going to call you but I was with Ashton and completely forgot," I said apologetically.

"Again, I repeat, what?"

"Sorry, Kay, I don't have time to go all in detail about it. I will tell you when I get home, I promise. I have to leave for my new job in twenty minutes so I am not late! I don't have anything to wear and was hoping you could help." Much to my surprise, Kacey instantly got out of bed and stood up. I stood there in shock that she was really up at five in the morning. Even when we were in college, she made sure to have her classes at eight or nine.

"What are you doing? We have to get going!" she practically yelled at me, turning on her bedroom light. She turned to her closet and started looking through it. "What kind of job is it?"

"An assistant. I am the boss's assistant," I said, hoping she wouldn't ask who the boss was. I didn't have time for her to start freaking out on me.

"I hope you know the moment you get home I will be expecting details about everything that happened yesterday." She turned to give me a pointed look. I nodded, not expecting anything less. "Okay, here." She threw a couple of items at me. I was grateful that I had put on a bra and panties on underneath my towel before coming to get her. Even though Kacey and I have seen each other naked, I would rather not stand there in the nude.

Seeing that she threw me a pencil skirt and come kind of blouse, I dropped the towel to slide into the black skirt while Kacey looked for shoes. I was never more grateful that we were the same size until now. I'd never worn a pencil skirt before and it felt weird hugging my butt and thighs. I slipped on the white blouse, glad I wore a white bra today.

"Here." Kacey handed me a black waist belt and pair of Louis Vuitton heels. I wobbled a little on the heels but found my footing. *This might be a long day.* Looking in the mirror on the side of her wall, I almost whistled. Wow, I looked pretty good. "Now let's do you hair and makeup." Kacey gripped my arm and pushed me onto the seat in front of her vanity. I sat still as she did her work. Times like these I loved that my best friend was a fashion expert. Not even ten minutes later Kacey set down her hair straightener and said I was done. "You look hot if I say so myself." She put her hands on her hips.

I looked in the mirror and almost gasped. Kacey had done a great job. My makeup looked almost natural, she had put a little bit of blush on my cheeks, and gave my eyes an almost smoky look with black and silver making my gray eyes pop more. She had me in a light shade of pink lipstick. My brown hair was straightened with a little bit of wave at the ends. All in all, I looked very good.

"Thank you, Kay!" I got up and hugged her. She hugged me back then pulled away quickly.

"You better get going; it's almost five thirty."

"Shit! Thank you so much! See you when I get home," I said as I practically ran out of her room and to mine to grab my bag. I grabbed my phone and my bag that already had the things I needed in it. I walked out the door with another bye to Kacey, but I knew she was already back in bed. I quickly made my way out of my building and to the curb for a cab.

I got a cab pretty quick. I didn't know the address of Ashton's work, so I just told the driver the building name.

"Wow, nice place to be working at." He whistled as he drove in the direction we needed.

"Is it? This is my first day," I told him.

"Well good for you." He sent me a smile through the review mirror.

"Miller Industries is a huge building and very well known here in New York. I've driven plenty of people there and they all seem to like working there."

"Thanks. That sounds good so hopefully, I will like it there too." Checking the time on the

131

dashboard, I saw it was only 5:35 and we looked to be almost there. "Is there a coffee place near there?" I asked. Maybe I could stop by and grab something before going in, maybe get Ashton something.

"Oh yes, there is a great little place about two buildings down on the left. Best coffee in downtown," he said. Just then, he came to a stop in front of the building.

"I'll have to go there. How much is it?" I asked, reaching into my bag for my wallet.

"It's on the house, little lady," the driver said turning in his chair to smile at me. His smile wasn't perverted or creepy; it was sincere.

"What? Oh no, I have to pay something," I protested.

"No need. I have a daughter your age and you remind me of her. Have a good first day." I shot him a huge smile.

"Well thank you! I hope you have a good day too," I said, getting out. *He was super nice.* I watched him drive away. Knowing I better hurry, I walked to the left like the man had said and came to a stop in front of what looked to be a cute place called Sunrise Cafe. I pushed open the door and saw the place was semi-packed already. The moment I pushed through the door, I was engulfed in the smell of fresh ground coffee. I breathed it in deeply, loving that smell. In an almost euphoric state, I walked to the front counter.

"Hello. What can I get you?" a cute guy asked, walking to the cashier. He was tall, maybe six-foot-one, and had shaggy blonde hair that hung on his forehead. He had gorgeous green eyes, and a wide white smile.

"Hi. I'll have a hazelnut latte, and…" I looked at the menu wondering what Ashton would want. "Just a regular coffee, I think," I said sending him a smile.

"Anything else I can get the pretty lady?" he asked. I looked at his name tag and saw his name was Jack. I blushed and shook my head. "What name to put on the cups?"

"Layla," I said as I watched him write it down.

"Pretty name." I couldn't help but blush again. I thanked him quietly.

"That will be seven-fifty." My eyebrows rose in surprise. *Wow, that's pretty cheap,* I thought. I fished out a ten-dollar bill.

"Keep the change," I said.

"Well, thank you." He shot me a smile. I sent one back and stood off to the side as he made my drinks. A few minutes later, he handed them over to me. "Hope to see you around, Layla." I gripped the cups in my hands.

"You too." As I left the cafe, I looked down at my cup and saw a smiley face written next to my name. I shook my head and laughed softly as I walked through the front doors of Miller Industries. I was surprised to see there was already tons of people here and it wasn't even six yet. Not knowing where I was supposed to go, I walked up to the reception desk. A blonde sat there typing on her computer and looked to be angrily talking to someone on her phone ear piece. As I walked up to her, I saw she was pretty but her face had way too much makeup on, and there was something about her face that screamed bitch.

"Uh, hi," I said as soon as she ended the call she was on.

"Yes?" she asked but didn't even look in my direction.

"I am new here and was wondering where Ash— Mr. Miller's office is?" I said, correcting myself at the last minute.

"Sorry, but I am not allowed to give that information out. Do you have a card?" She finally turned to look at me. She stared at me with a pair of cold blue eyes.

"A card?" I asked, not knowing what she was talking about.

"See, all employees get a card or badge that lets us know you work here. You definitely don't and you just want to see Mr. Miller. So, you can just leave now," she said, dismissing me with a wave of her hand and going back to her computer.

Excuse me?

"I am *new* so I do not have a card. That is why I have to see Mr. Miller. I am his new assistant," I said, trying hard not to sound rude. That seemed to get her attention and she turned back to me. Her ruby red lips pursed as she glared at me.

"Nice try. If you're his assistant, then the world has come to an end," she said in one of the snottiest voices I had ever heard. I had to hold myself back from hitting her. She talked down to me as if I were some low-class person.

"I—" Before I could get something out, another voice came from beside me. I turned my head and saw a pretty blonde girl next to me. Her hair was cut in a cute bob style and she was pretty short, standing at five-three maybe. She looked to be about my age.

"Cecilia, don't be rude. I believe her," the girl said, coming to my defense. *So, Cecilia, that's her name. No wonder she's a bitch.* "Hi, I am Neena Brown." She held out her hand for me to shake and sent me a smile. I instantly liked this girl.

"Hi, I am Layla Kingston." I shook her hand.

"Nice to meet you. I will show you to Mr. Miller's office." She lightly grabbed my elbow and pulled me away from Cecilia and to the elevators across the room.

"Ignore Cecilia. She's a bitch and thinks she owns the place," Neena said with a roll of her eyes. I stopped, a giggle from escaping my lips. Yep, I liked this girl. We were able to squeeze into an elevator before it closed.

"I work at the front desk as well, so if you ever need anything just ask for me," Neena continued. "Mr. Miller's office is on the thirtieth floor. There aren't many people on the level; it's mostly just for him and his receptionist. Practically all the levels are different sections of the company. You have the tech people on floor twenty, where they take care of anything with technology. You have marketing on the twenty-fifth floor, and so on and so forth. I don't want to waste a lot of time going over those floors because you probably won't need to go there." Slowly the elevator started to empty, until it was only me and Neena and we had three more floors to go.

"Can I ask you a question?" I asked Neena,

hoping she would say yes.

"Of course. Shoot."

"Do you know anything about Mr. Miller?" I figured this was a good opportunity to find out more about Ashton and how he runs his business. I'd never seen this side of him and wanted a little heads up before going in blind.

"Well, he is very successful. His family built this company from the ground up. It was mainly Mr. Miller who made the company what it is today. Don't get me wrong, his father was great but Mr. Miller has made the company larger than anyone else's and has brought on twice as many beneficiaries as his father. He is a great businessman but can be very ruthless when he wants to be. But I am warning you, he is quite the charmer," Neena said. *Oh, I already know that.* No need to tell Neena that I'd already seen his charming side.

"I wish I could tell you he is a sweet guy but in reality, he isn't. He uses women for sex then leaves them. But sadly, the women here still fall to his feet whenever he walks by." The way she was talking about him wasn't at all how I have come to know Ashton. "Oops, sorry, I probably shouldn't have said that to his new assistant," Neena said, shooting me an apologetic smile. *I guess things aren't always what they seem.* The elevator doors chimed open and we stepped out. Now I was starting to become nervous as I followed Neena. We passed a lot of cubicles that already had people in them working on stuff. She clearly knew how this place worked.

"How do you know these things?" I asked.

"Oh, everyone around here gossips. I've worked here for four years now and know the ins and outs. Being usually quiet, I pick up on what everyone is saying." She shrugged. "Okay, here you go. This is Mr. Miller's receptionist, Judy. She will take you from here. If you need anything, just call downstairs for me. It was great meeting you. Hopefully, we can talk again soon." With that, she left and headed back to the elevators.

"Hello, you must be Ms. Kingston I assume?" Judy asked, standing up from her desk. She was an older woman with white hair starting to show through the brown. She had a kind smile and pretty light brown eyes. Just by looking at her, I knew I would like her. I was just surprised that Ashton had someone like her as his receptionist instead of some hot young girl or even someone like Cecilia from downstairs.

"Hi, yes I am," I said kindly, shaking her hand.

"Ashton told me this morning when he walked in that we should be expecting you." Judy said his name as if she were talking about her son. I could tell Judy loved Ashton. "I hope he doesn't scare you off like his other assistants. They didn't last a day, but of course, those girls were bimbos. I was actually surprised to hear he hired someone new." I couldn't help but let out a laugh as she called Ashton's last assistants bimbos.

"Hopefully I will be sticking around longer than them," I said once I had stopped laughing. She sent me a smile.

"You can go in; he's been expecting you." She gestured to the door a few feet behind her desk.

"When you're done, I'll show you to your new office and explain what you'll be doing. That boy doesn't know how to give instructions slowly or in depth." She shook her head but then nodded at me. Sending her a smile, I walked over to the door. My hands shook slightly with the coffee in them. *Do I knock then go in? Or should I just walk in?* I decided to knock then go in. Balancing the coffees in one hand, I tapped on the wood door and grabbed the handle. *It's now or* never. Hearing Ashton's deep voice saying "Come in," I opened the door with shaky legs.

Chapter 14

Layla

I walked through Ashton's office and nudged the door shut with my hip. Glancing around, I tried not to gasp at how nice his office looked. The walls were a dark blue with a black leather couch on one side. He had two huge windows that overlooked downtown New York. Everything about it screamed Ashton to me.

"Good morning," I said, breaking the silence. His carpet muffled the clicks of my heels as I walked to his desk. Setting his cup down in front of him, I looked at the two nice chairs that sat in front of his desk. Not knowing it if was okay to sit, I slowly sat on the edge of one of them.

"Good morning," he replied. He looked up and saw the cup I had sat down and a small smile graced his lips. "Coffee?"

"Uh, yes. I didn't know what you liked so I just got just a regular coffee," I answered, feeling my cheeks tinting with pink.

"Well thank you." He took a sip of it. I mimicked him and sat there silently, waiting for him to tell me what I'll be doing.

"Okay, since you are now my new assistant, I have a lot for you to do. Here." He handed over what looked like a phone to me. I looked down at it and saw it was the new iPhone. I gingerly held it, not knowing what to do with such a nice phone. I mean I didn't have a stupid phone, but mine was an old iPhone that I got years ago. "On there are all my appointments, clients' numbers, and my entire schedule. I advise you don't lose that like you did your real phone or we both will be in a lot of trouble." I bowed my head in embarrassment, but still nodded.

"The job isn't too hard, but it will take a little bit to get used to. I expect everything to be done on time. When I have meetings, I also expect you to be there to take notes then later you will review them with me. Some nights we still stay later than others." The way Ashton was talking to me, I knew he was in business mode. "I want to let you know right now that I don't tolerate laziness, ignorance, or incompetence. My employees know what they are doing and make sure it gets it done fast and right. Now." He stood up and made his way around his big desk. He stood in front of me making me look up. "Layla, I do not mean to be rude to you, but this is my company and I will do anything for it to succeed; I need you to see that."

I nodded at him, understanding. I knew this was his business. I shouldn't expect any special treatment and I wouldn't take any. I did not want to be known around the office as the girl who had probably slept with the boss and got the job that way.

"I definitely understand, Ash—I mean Mr. Miller, sir," I said.

"Good. I have a meeting at eight, so meet me in conference room 201 and be early. I don't want my assistant to show up late," Ashton said. With that, he nodded at me and went back to his seat. Taking that as my cue to leave, I got up and left his office shutting the door behind me.

"Ms. Kingston, you can follow me to your new office," Judy said, leading me just a few feet away. She came to a stop in front of a pretty big office with glass walls.

"This is yours." I walked through the door and almost whistled. It looked amazing. I had never had an office before, and it looked like it was straight out of a magazine or TV show. A big mahogany desk sat straight ahead with an Apple computer. On one side of the office was a dark blue couch that looked really comfortable and a couple of chairs almost like Ashton's.

"Wow, this is mine?" I asked, sliding my bag off my shoulder and setting it gently on the desk, my desk.

"Yes, it is. Now, what did Ashton tell you?" Judy asked beside me.

"This phone has all his appointments, meetings, and clients' numbers in it. That how he doesn't like laziness, ignorance, and incompetence. That's about it," I said, trying to remember if he said anything about what my job actually entails.

"That's what I thought," Judy said, shaking her head. "Okay, well, as his assistant, you will take care of all his meetings; meaning you will set them up, know who is coming and what they want, and make sure that Ashton knows exactly what they are about. You also will look over any files, paperwork, anything that Ashton already did or wants you to do. I am not going to lie to you; this job isn't easy, even though Ashton said it is. There is a lot of work that needs to get done every day. But I have faith that you will be able to get it done." She smiled.

"Now I know he has a meeting at eight, so here is a list of things you need to do before then and before lunch. You have to copy the files needed for the meeting so every person has a copy. Thankfully it isn't a big meeting; it is just a company one with every supervisor from every floor discussing what has been going on and what needs improving. The copies are just of the numbers from the last six months and everything that has been going on in each department. Nothing too big. Thankfully, today there isn't a lot to be done. Everything on the list isn't too hard and should be able to get done in just a few hours." I looked down at the list Judy had given me. My eyes almost bulged out of my head when I saw how many things were on there. *A little? Yeah, right.*

"If you need anything, I will be more than happy to help. I would start right with these right now. The copier is down the hall first door on the left." She put her hand on a stack of papers. "You will need about twenty to twenty-five copies. Wouldn't hurt to make extras." I nodded, a little dazed. "You'll be fine, honey," she said, patting my shoulder and leaving the room.

Okay, I can do this. How hard can it be?

***

Two hours later, I took back what I thought earlier. I was walking as fast as I could in my almost five-inch heels, toward conference room 201. My arms were filled with about thirty copies for the meeting. It was fifteen minutes to eight and I was behind. I didn't think it would take me so long to make copies. At first, I couldn't find the copy room, then the printer was so confusing it took me a good ten minutes trying to figure it out, and finally I printed the copies; I then had to staple them and put them in their own binders. After doing that, I had to call all the supervisors of each department and make sure they remembered the meeting was at eight.

Now I was hurrying to make sure I had everything set up before they all started to trickle in. Plus, I didn't want to embarrass myself in front of Ashton. I made my way blindly to conference room 201, not knowing where it was. I was hoping I was heading the right way, and if not, I would be late. I could have asked Judy, but I didn't want to bother her and I wanted to do this on my own. Thankfully, I saw the number 201 ahead of me. Letting out a breath of relief, I quickly hurried over to it and shouldered the door open. I was now very thankful that I had gotten coffee before I came here. I knew before the end of the day I would be exhausted.

Setting down folders on the empty table, I then

put them on the empty chairs that sat all along the wall of the conference room. Carrying the extra copies, I set them in a seat that was off to the side where I thought Ashton would sit. I glanced around trying to see if I missed anything. Seeing a pitcher sitting in the middle of the table and glasses in front of the chairs, I realized I guess I better fill it up, even though I had no idea how to do so. But before I could make a move to grab it, the office doors opened and people started coming in. None of the supervisors paid me any attention, chatting away with one another and finding a chair to sit in. One girl passed by me and her shoulder hit mine, making me stumble in my heels. Luckily, I caught myself before I fell making an embarrassment of myself.

Since Ashton hadn't come yet, I decided I should just go sit in my chair and wait for the meeting to start. Once I sat down, I held the pile of folders on my lap along with my new work phone, and a notebook and pen for notes. I didn't exactly know what Ashton meant by notes, so I just thought if anyone said any ideas or spoke up, I'd write it down. In all honesty, I was worried about being here since I knew nothing about this company. All I knew was that very rich people invested in us, and that there were a lot of company buildings all over the US and Europe. *Better research what the company is about later.* I glanced at the clock straight ahead of me and saw it was past eight. *Where's Ashton?* Just then, the door opened and in he walked.

The moment he stepped through the door, everyone quieted and turned to look at him, me included. I hadn't noticed what he was wearing earlier, but now I did. His wide shoulders were fitted in a black suit jacket, and beneath that was a white button-up shirt with a deep maroon color tie. He had on black dress slacks and black dress shoes as well. His hair was brushed back, with a slight curl to it. A five o'clock shadow graced his well-defined cheekbones and jaw line. I tried not to gawk openly at him, but it was hard. I could see all the other women in the room staring at him as well.

His presence seemed to take up the entire room, making the room extra quiet. He walked confidently to the head of the table, which was right in front of me where I thought he would sit. Nodding at a few people, he walked toward me and sent me a simple nod. I tried not to feel slightly hurt that he didn't smile at me and that he just nodded at me like everyone else. I knew he wouldn't acknowledge me while at work, but I still felt somewhat hurt. With a jolt, I frowned at myself for feeling hurt. Why would I, when nothing was even happening between us? *You're hurt because you want something to happen between you.* I wanted to deny that but I knew it was futile. I did want something to happen between us and I knew that was wrong because nothing ever could. I was now his assistant. I couldn't be involved with my boss. While I was talking to myself in my head, Ashton had started the meeting already. Shaking my head, I forced myself to focus on what people were saying and not the handsome man in front of me.

The meeting went by in a blur with my taking notes on practically everything. Before I knew it,

Ashton stood up and said goodbye to everyone. Glancing at the clock, I saw it was about 9:45, the meeting having been an hour and forty-five minutes. I dropped my pen and shook out my hand as I looked at what I had written down. I had filled up about three pages of notes and my handwriting was sloppy almost unreadable by the last page. As everyone started filing out, I stood up, one arm carrying the extra folders and the other smoothing down my skirt. A few people lingered in the room talking to one another, but I saw Ashton was leaving so I quickly followed him wanting to ask him something.

With his long strides, I didn't catch up with him until he reached his office.

"Mr. Miller?" I asked, trying to not sound out of breath as I came to a stop in front of him. *Man, I need to work out more often.*

"Yes?" He turned and looked down at me. Even in my heels I only reached his chest, maybe shoulders.

"Um, I was wondering what you wanted me to do with these extra folders, and about the notes I took at the meeting."

"Keep one so you can file it with the others, but the rest you can throw away. Later, we can discuss the notes. What do I have going on before lunch?" he asked in a rush. His voice was so hard and business-like that I wanted to almost slap him and get him to stop talking to me like that, but I knew I couldn't.

"You have nothing until noon where you have to go and meet a Mr.—" I scrambled to think of his last name. "Terry! At some restaurant called Cucina Italian," I said. Ashton just nodded at me and opened his office door, then shutting it behind him. I stood there, shocked. *Okay.* I recalled what he said about filing the meeting's data work.

"Judy?" I called her name as I walked over to her desk.

"Yes, Ms. Kingston?" She looked up from her computer.

"Oh, just call me Layla. I don't like being called Ms. Kingston." I didn't like being called that because it reminded me of my mother and I didn't want to go down that road.

"Okay, Layla."

"Mr. Miller said I need to file one of these folders. What does he mean by that?" I asked.

"You have a filing cabinet in your office and that's where all files for meetings and conferences go. Ashton likes to keep those data pages and meeting stuff close by in case something happens. The other girls before you didn't do a good job at filing and I've tried reorganizing it, but I haven't had time, so it is probably a mess," Judy said, sending me an apologetic smile. I just nodded back and headed to my office to drop off these extra folders.

Great, just great. I tried remembering if I had seen a staff lounging area where I could maybe recycle these. *I think I saw one down the hall on the way to the conference room.* After a few missed turns, I found it. To my surprise, it was actually pretty nice for a staff room. A fridge was on one side, with a sink right by it. A few coffee tables and chairs were scattered around and a pretty comfy-looking couch sat against a wall. Out of the corner of my eye, I saw two bins that were labeled garbage and recycling. My heels clicked on the tile floor as I walked to the recycle bin and threw in the nine or so extra folders. *There goes all my hard work,* I thought almost bitterly.

"Hello?" a pretty deep, accented voice said from behind me. I turned and saw an attractive guy leaning against the door frame to the room. He had kind of short dirty blonde hair, with a few days'-old scruff along his face. From here, I couldn't see what color his eyes were but I knew they would be pretty. His jaw line was so defined I bet it could cut cheese or glass. He had on a white button-up dress shirt with a thin blue tie. His sleeves were rolled up halfway, showing his forearms. And he had on a pair of black slacks as well. So, all in all, he looked hot.

"H-Hi," I stuttered out. *Damn it, Layla, talk normal!*

"Are you new? I don't think I have seen you around before?" the guy said, walking away from the wall toward me. He had an Australian accent that could make any girl fall for him.

"No, I am new. I just started today," I said, liking his accent. "I am Layla, Layla Kingston."

"Nice to meet you. I am Liam, Liam Bennett." He stuck his hand out for me to shake once he came to a stop in front of me. I looked up at him, another very tall guy. He had a pair of really blue eyes.

"You too. Do you work on this floor?" I asked once I was done staring at his pretty face.

"Yeah, I do. I do statistical analysis and data reconfiguration," Liam said. I stared at him blankly having no idea what that meant. "I find and make the company's statistical numbers. I basically find what we are spending and make sure we don't go over, and that everything works smoothly with our numbers and money."

"Oh...cool," I said, nodding even though I was still confused by what he did.

"What do you do?" he asked.

"I am Mr. Miller's new assistant." After the words left my lips, I saw Liam look at me in surprise. "What?"

"Nothing, I just never would have guessed you as Mr. Miller's assistant." He shrugged at me.

"Why not?" *Did I not look smart enough, or was my outfit not right?* I wondered.

"You just look smarter than the others. I would have figured you to be in a more...sophisticated position instead." I felt a blush coming on but I forced it down.

"Well, thank you. I don't mind being his assistant though. I'm just happy for the job," I said, smiling at him.

He opened his mouth but a ringing interrupted him. He shot me a small smile.

"Sorry, I better go. It was nice meeting you. Hopefully, I'll see you around." He sent me a smirk and left. All I could do was chuckle and head back to my office.

I shut the door behind me and headed to my desk. I plopped down in my chair and let out a sigh. It was only ten and I was ready to go home. My feet hurt, I was starting to get a headache, and I was hungry. I softly pushed my chair back and forth with my heel as I finally looked around my office. I saw in the corner the filing cabinet Judy was talking about. Groaning softly, I saw pieces of paper sticking out and the door opened slightly. I was not looking forward to having to refile all that was in there. Deciding that I had time to do that later, I turned to my computer and started playing around on it seeing if there was stuff I needed on there. At least I had a Mac laptop at home or I wouldn't know how this one worked.

After about thirty minutes of playing around on it, I knew I had to start on the filing. It would probably take me a couple of days to go through it and put it in order. With a quick glance out through my windows, I slipped off my shoes and padded to the file cabinet in my bare feet. I instantly felt one of my problems go away as the pain in my feet slowly went away. With a quiet groan, I pulled open the cabinet and went to work.

***

Two and a half hours later, I threw down whatever was in my hand and rubbed my head. I had only made a small dent in the documents. My office floor was littered with papers and I had no idea what most of the stuff was of even about. My headache was even worse and my stomach growled loudly. Grabbing my phone, I saw it about 12:30. *Do I get a lunch?* Knowing it couldn't hurt, I slipped back on my shoes, fixed my skirt, grabbed my bag, and headed to go ask Judy. I could really use something to eat and drink.

"Hi Judy," I said once I got to her desk.

"Hello. I didn't know you were still here. I thought you left with Ashton." I stared at her wide-eyed as I remembered Ashton had a lunch meeting at noon and I forgot to remind him. *Shit!*

"Oh, um, yeah I decided to stay back and finish what I was doing anyways," I said quickly, lying. "I was just wondering if I get a lunch break. I am starving."

"Yes, you do. Most leave around noon or so and get back at one. Go and get something to eat. Ashton probably won't be back until 1:30 anyways."

"Thanks," I said, smiling at her. Giving her a small wave, I walked toward the elevator and clicked the button. The doors opened a second later and I got in and headed for the ground floor. A loud "hold the door" was yelled at me, so I quickly put my hand on the closing elevator doors. A second later, Liam came to a stop in front of me.

"Layla!" he said, smiling at me and coming to stand next to me. I could smell his cologne, and I tried to conceal myself from sniffing the air every few seconds. *He smells really good, though not as good as Ashton,* I thought.

"Hi Liam," I said back.

"Are you heading to go eat?" I nodded, looking into his blue eyes. "Mind if I join you? I know a great place to eat," he said.

I thought about it for a minute as we slowly descended to the lobby. I didn't know a good place to eat. Plus, I didn't like eating alone somewhere I'd never been.

"Sure," I said with a smile as I accepted. *What could it hurt?*

Chapter 15

Layla

I stood next to Liam in the exact same place I got coffee this morning, Sunrise Cafe. We stood behind a few people waiting to order.

"This place has really good food, and it's quick if you're in a rush," Liam said, looking down at me. Even with my heels, I was shorter than everyone. We made it to the front and Liam immediately sprouted off his order to the younger girl. She shot him a small, shy smile as she clicked it into the computer. I waited for him to finish, but Liam didn't move.

"Are you going to order?" he asked.

"Yeah, but just waiting for you."

"No, I am paying."

"No, I won't let you pay," I said, shaking my head. "I can pay for myself."

"Nope, not going to happen. Think of it as your 'welcome to your first day' lunch." Seeing as he wouldn't budge, I rolled my eyes. I ordered a

Caribbean salad and just got water. "That's all you're getting?" Liam asked as he handed over money to the girl.

"Yeah, it sounds really good," I said, shrugging. The salad had mandarin oranges, Chinese croutons, chicken, shredded almonds, and a delicious-sounding dressing.

The girl handed him a number stand and Liam steered me toward an empty table by the window. I sat across from him and glanced out the window. People walked by at a brisk pace trying to get to where they are going.

"Thank you for lunch," I said, sending Liam a smile.

"You are welcome." He smiled back. Before awkward silence could wrap around us, I asked him a question.

"So, you were born in Australia?" I asked, leaning forward and resting my head on my hands staring at him.

"I was. I was born in a small town just a little outside of Sydney. I lived there until university, when I got accepted into NYU on a basketball scholarship," Liam said.

"Wow. You must have been really good at basketball to get a scholarship at NYU. Did you just graduate?" He couldn't have been more than two years older than I was.

"Yeah, I graduated almost 3 years ago. I'm twenty-five."

"What did you major in?"

"Well, at first I didn't know what to major in. I thought I'd make my way through the four years then get drafted maybe. But my second year in, I got hurt, really hurt, and had to quit basketball. That's when I figured I better start going for something else. That's when I decided to major in business and math."

"I am sorry; that sounds terrible," I said and I meant it. It would suck having all your dreams crash around you in just an instant. "But at least you got a good degree and are working at a nice place," I said, trying to sound bright.

"You're right about that." He chuckled. Just then, someone came with our food and set it in front of us. My salad looked really good and was huge. My stomach growled the moment the plate came to rest in front of me. I blushed and shot Liam an embarrassed smile. He stared at me in amusement then shook his head.

"Someone is hungry." He grabbed the sandwich he got.

"Yeah, I am. I didn't get a chance to eat this morning." I started eating my salad and was surprised by how good it was. We ate in silence for the next few minutes before Liam asked me something.

"So, how about you? Where did you go to college? Major?" he asked.

"Well, I grew up about thirty minutes away from here. I went to NYU as well, and just graduated almost two years ago too, and I'm twenty-three. I majored in Journalism," I said.

"Wow, we barely missed each other. Not surprised we didn't see each other since the campus is so large. But Journalism, that's pretty cool. What made you go into that?"

"I honestly don't know. I like to write and I like English, so it was an obvious choice I guess."

We talked back and forth while we ate our lunch. Liam was easy to talk to and I could feel myself relaxing around him. I knew that I had at least one friend at work now. Looking down at my phone, I saw it was way past 1 o'clock and I wanted to be back before Ashton.

"I think we better head back. It's almost one thirty," I said, cleaning up my lunch.

"You're right. Here, let me take that," Liam said, grabbing my plate and going to the garbage. While he threw away our stuff, I slipped my bag on my shoulder, grabbed my phone, and fixed my outfit. "Ready?"

I nodded and followed Liam out the door and toward the building.

"Thanks for lunch, Liam," I said, smiling over at him.

"No problem. You're great company. I'm glad we'll be working together," he said sincerely. We walked through the doors of the building. I saw Neena and shot her a small wave. She waved back but was blocked as someone came up to the desk to talk to her. Silently, we stood and waited for the elevator, people standing around us. With a bing, the doors opened and we were immediately surrounded by people. Liam and I were smashed against the side of the wall as more and more people trickled in. Liam's arm wrapped itself around my waist and pulled me back against him so my back was to his chest. I could feel warmth radiating off of his arm and through my blouse. I blushed and looked down, not knowing what to do with his arm around me.

Slowly, people exited off their floors but Liam still kept me pressed against him. We got closer to the thirtieth floor and we stood in the elevator with about seven other people. That awkward elevator silence wrapped around us all. I resisted the urge to babble about nothing as we got closer. Thankfully, a few minutes later the doors opened to our floor. Liam held me back as everyone left and slowly retracted his arm. My skin felt hot. I couldn't help but wonder why he did that. Lost in my thoughts, I didn't notice we had stopped a little bit ahead of Ashton's office and Judy's desk, until I practically ran into Liam. I stumbled and his hand shot out, steadying me.

"Sorry, I guess I was lost in thought."

"No worries. Thank you for letting me intrude on your lunch."

"Thank you for intruding. I wouldn't have had any fun if I was alone."

"Good. I better go. It was nice having lunch with you, Layla. If you need anything, let me know. I am only down the hall. Feel free to drop by anytime. See you later." He smiled his pretty smile at me then walked off. My name sounded so cool with his accent. I turned around to head to Judy, my relaxed feeling fading away as I thought of what I had to do this afternoon. I didn't get very far before I ran into what felt like a brick wall.

"Oomph." I glanced up and looked at a not very happy Ashton. His jaw was clenched and his blue eyes were narrowed and looked darker. I tried not to flinch at how he was staring at me; it was almost like I did something wrong but I hadn't. *You forgot to remind him about his lunch meeting.* "Uh, hi," I said, stammering.

"My office. Now." With that, he turned and strode to his office. He held the door open and looked at me. He gave me a look that said *right now*. I gulped audibly, and with shaky legs walked to his office, I slid by him and my shoulder rubbed against his chest. Ashton followed me and shut the door with a click. For some reason, that click sounded so ominous. I slowly sunk into the chair I sat in earlier and waited for Ashton to talk. He sat in his chair and stared at me. For a good three minutes, we sat there staring at each other. Me wondering what was going to happen, and him like I had done something to royally piss him off.

"Nice weather we are having, isn't it?" I said, breaking the thick tension in the room. Ashton still sat glaring down at me.

"I have to pee," I blurted. My eyes widened as soon as the words left my mouth. *Really? You have to pee? You couldn't have said anything else, could you?* The awkward turtle that I am was starting to burst through. It was one of those moments when the urge to pee came up at the most inopportune time. Like right before a race, just as the announcer starts counting down, you realize you have to use the bathroom but by then it's too late. Then, as you run, the feeling disappears.

Ashton's eyebrows rose up and his face softened slightly but was still hard.

"Why did you have lunch with Mr. Bennett?" Ashton asked suddenly. I didn't expect him to talk, just to sit there and make me squirm.

"What?"

"Why were you having lunch with Mr. Bennett, Layla?" he asked again, his voice hard.

"Why does it matter?" I said, feeling slightly angry at how he was treating me.

"Because it just does! You are supposed to be doing your job instead of flirting with another co-worker." Flirting? I couldn't flirt, and when I did try to, I sounded like Ross from *Friends* talking about how gas is made. The only person I had ever flirted with was Ashton, and for some reason, it just came out around him. But still, even then it wasn't the greatest flirting.

"I wasn't flirting with him. I was being polite because he offered to take to me lunch when I don't know anyone. You think I would flirt with someone at work, and on my first day?" I said, feeling hurt. He sighed and ran a hand down his face.

"No, I guess not. I just don't want you to spend two hours at lunch with him when I need you here." He leaned back in his chair.

"Two hours? I was only gone almost an hour."

"Around noon I went looking for you since you never came by my office. When I couldn't find you, I figured you had left for lunch as do most at noon."

"I was in my office refiling what your stupid other assistants didn't do. And because you didn't tell me anything of what my job entails, I did not know I could have lunch until twelve thirty. You can't get mad at me for getting something to eat with another co-worker. You should be happy I am meeting new people here and that I get along with them." I could feel myself getting angry. The way he'd been treating me and now with him being angry that I went to lunch with someone, I felt myself about to snap. I stood up knowing I better not be in the same room as him until both of us had cooled off little.

"I better get back to work. There is a lot I have to do. Whenever you want to go over those notes, let me know." With that, I left his office and headed to mine. I didn't do anything wrong and I wasn't going to sit there and listen to Ashton yelling at me for something stupid. It wasn't like I kissed Liam or felt him up in front of anyone. Shaking my head, I shut my office door and looked around my messy floor. Setting my bag down, I grabbed my work phone and looked through it, looking to see if there was anything I really needed to do. Seeing nothing on my phone and a few things on the list Judy gave me, I got to work on those and refiling, hoping it would occupy my mind for a while.

***

Four p.m. rolled around and I was just sorting the files on the ground of oldest to newest when a knock sounded on my door. I shouted for them to come in and kept doing what I was doing. My headache was back and my back hurt from leaning forward for hours. I heard my door click shut and glanced up. Ashton leaned against the door looking down at me with amusement in his eyes. I felt guilt flow through me, and I knew I acted slightly childish.

I slowly stood but being the clumsy person I was, I somehow managed to trip on a pile of paper. I closed my eyes waiting for impact on the ground but after a second, I didn't feel anything. I opened them. A hard chest was right in front of me and a pair of strong arms wrapped around my waist. Looking up, I saw Ashton had caught me before I hit the ground. My cheeks turned pink and untangled myself from his arms.

"Sorry," I said, ignoring the feeling of wanting him to wrap his arms back around me.

"You're so clumsy." He smirked down at me and stuck his hands in his pockets. The way he did it made his shoulders come in slightly, and I swear I saw his tricep muscles bulge through his suit jacket. *Ashton, why are you so hot?*

"And I don't have my shoes on either," I joked back. He shot me another smirk then stepped back.

"I came to see if you were busy. I wanted to go over those notes from this morning's meeting."

"Yeah, one second, let me clean this up," I said. Not thinking about it, I turned and squatted to pick up the papers littering the floor. After stacking them in the order I wanted, I laid them inside the cabinet and shut it. I would finish tomorrow. I felt Ashton's eyes on me as I worked and I self-consciously pulled my skirt down. Straightening up, I slipped on my heels again and grabbed the folder on my desk from this morning. Turning around, I saw Ashton staring at me with a hungry look in his eyes. His blue eyes were almost black, and his jaw and fist

161

were clenched.

"Ready?" I asked him, walking toward him.

"Uh…yes." He shook his head, seeming to clear his thoughts. Inside, I was pleased I got that reaction out of him. Instead of his usual calm and collected look, he actually looked flustered. Sending him a small smirk, I slid past him, purposely rubbing against him as I passed. Payback for being rude to me all day. I walked to his office and heard his footsteps behind me. He closed the door and walked to his desk. He once again had his calm and collected face back on. I slid the folder and my notes across the desk to him.

Ashton read the through my notes and he looked pretty pleased. He set them down after five minutes and looked at me.

"Good job. Were you at all lost during the meeting?"

"A little bit, but I figured it out while everyone talked," I said honestly. I knew tonight I would have to do some serious research on everything about Miller's Industries. I did not want to go in blind if there were any important meetings this week.

"Good. The meetings are held about every month so I know what each department has going on and that we are all on the same page." I nodded. A few seconds of silence surrounded us. "Layla, I—"

"Ashton, I—" I started at the same time. I smiled at him then gestured for him to go first.

"I am sorry for getting upset with you earlier. I shouldn't have accused you of flirting with Mr. Bennett. When I couldn't find you, I kind of got worried since I hadn't heard from you. I promise I won't do that again." He was sincere. I held back a smile that he was the first to apologize.

"I'm sorry too, Ashton. I shouldn't have lost track of time and reminded you of your meeting as well, or at least texted you. And I am sorry I yelled at you then stormed out," I said.

"It's okay. I realize this is your first day and I've dumped a lot of stuff on you that you don't know how to do. I will try and be better at that as well."

"Thank you," I said, smiling. He sent me one of his rare half-smiles back.

"How about, to make it up to you, I take you to dinner?" Ashton offered, the look on his face almost nervous. Small butterflies filled my stomach as I thought about eating dinner with Ashton again.

"Sure, I'd like that." I bit my bottom lip.

"Good. Let's go. There's nothing else left to do here." He stood up and walked to my chair and held his hand out for me to take. I put my small hand in his big one and let him pull me up and to the door.

"Just let me grab my stuff from my office." I shot him a quick smile. I walked back to my office and grabbed my bag and phone. Turning the light off and shutting the door, I walked back to Ashton who was saying goodbye to Judy.

"Have a good night, Layla," Judy said once I stopped beside Ashton.

"You too, Judy. Thanks for all the help today."

"No problem, sweetie. Take care of her, Ashton," she said, her voice low in warning, and I looked at him. He nodded and put his hand on my lower back and guided me to the elevator. Since it was 4:30, people were starting to pack up their things and they stared at us as we walked by. I could bet there will be a rumor started by tomorrow about me sleeping with Ashton. Thankfully, the elevator came a second after Ashton hit the button and no one else got in with us.

As we rode down to the lobby, Ashton stood a little behind me with his hand on my lower back. I could feel the heat radiating off his hand and seeping through my thin blouse.

"By the way," Ashton whispered into my ear. His warm breath spreading goosebumps along my skin. "You look very hot in that outfit." Just as the words left his lips, the elevator dinged open and he sauntered out, a smirk on his gorgeous face.

Chapter 16

Layla

Dinner with Ashton turned out to be a lot of fun, making me forget about him being rude to me. The Mexican restaurant we were at was semi-fancy and people stared at us almost wondering why we were so dressed up.

"You've never been to a concert?" Ashton asked, looking at me like I was from outer space. I shook my head and took a sip of the margarita Ashton practically made me order.

"I never had time or the money to go." I shrugged. My parents never let me do anything besides go to school and work. It was a miracle if I could go hangout with Kacey once in a while. I only worked because my parents forced me to and then, when I got my paychecks they would take them. And of course, the money I worked for only went for alcohol and food for them, not me.

"Wow."

"What concerts have you been to?" I asked,

turning the topic away from me.

"I've been to ACDC, Counting Crows, U2, Sting, and a few others."

I stared at him then shook my head.

"What?"

"I just...I just can't see you going to a concert. You're so formal," I said, hoping I wouldn't offend him.

"I'll have you know I was a big partier in college and high school," he said almost proudly.

"Sure, you were," I said and rolled my eyes.

The rest of the night, we talked and relaxed. I learned that Ashton had a sister and that she was about my age. I learned what his mom did and that his dad stepped down from CEO only a year ago. When Ashton asked me about my family, I just vaguely answered. My parents were kind of dead beats. They do have good jobs. My father is an electric engineer, and my mother is a manager at a fancy restaurant in my hometown. How could two well-known people in my hometown abuse their child, I had no idea. From the outside, no one knew what my home life was like and my parents made sure to keep it that way. I was threatened multiple times if I told anyone they would made me suffer more than I ever have. They made sure that when they hit me it wouldn't be see or could be covered up buy a long sleeve shirt or makeup.

I thought Ashton started to pick up that I didn't want to talk to my parents because, only after a few questions, he switched the subject, and for that I was grateful. Kacey was the only person to know, even though she didn't know all of it, and I wanted to keep it that way.

Around six, Ashton drove me home seeing I was tired as I yawned every five minutes. Walking me to my door, he said a quick good night and kissed my forehead once again. As he walked away, I had to hold myself back from running after him and kissing him. I wanted to feel his soft and warm lips against mine again, but for some reason Ashton wouldn't go that far. Sighing, I twisted open my door knob and walked in.

"You're home," Kacey said out of nowhere, making me almost scream. It was almost like one of those scary movies. Kacey sat on the couch cross-legged and staring at me almost creepily. I could tell she had been waiting for me to come home and she had her interrogation face on. Her blue eyes were narrowed and her eyebrows drawn in. I gulped waiting for all her questions to start flying at me. I didn't have to wait too long before her mouth was moving a hundred miles per hour. I only caught a few of her questions, making me stand there staring at her confused. She finally took a deep breath.

"So, what happened? And don't you dare leave anything out." I slipped off my high heels and dropped my bag on the table, then I took a seat on the couch. Before I even sat down, I was telling Kacey everything from the moment I left the apartment yesterday morning to when I just walked through the door. For the first time, she sat there quietly listening to me and not making comments in-between. When I got to the part where Ashton was rude to me and then nice by taking me to dinner, I got confused.

"Kay, I don't know what to do. One second he is super sweet and caring, then the next his rude, curt, and doesn't care if he hurts me," I said, almost whining. "He seems almost bipolar."

"Layla, you keep forgetting that work Ashton is different than nice Ashton. Do you think he would be where he is right now by being nice? Things probably would have been a lot easier if you had met business Ashton before nice Ashton. You have to realize that at work he is going to be different to you, even though you are his PA," Kacey said.

"I know. It's just hard. When I see him at work and he's in is hot suits, I just want to jump him," I admitted embarrassedly.

"You know you can't date him now, right?"

"What?" I asked even though I knew what she meant.

"You know what I'm talking about. Do you want people to start thinking the only reason you got the job was because you slept with him? Now that you are his PA, you can't have him." Her words hurt but were true. I couldn't have anything to do with him romantically. "I am sorry, Lay," she said when she saw the look on my face.

"No, it's fine." I shook my head. "I don't like him, Kay. I mean, I can't deny that is he isn't attractive but I don't like him like that," I lied, although I didn't sound convincing at all. Even though I had only known Ashton for a week, I already felt something for him. Kacey just stared at me giving me a look.

"Layla, I don't want you to get your hopes up. You have to remember that Ashton is a womanizer as well. I just don't want you to get hurt."

The rest of the night, Kacey's words kept running through my mind. *He's a womanizer.* What if he was just using me? That I was just his flavor of the week? Later that night, as I sat in bed researching the company on my laptop, I thought of Ashton. I didn't want to be just a fling or his flavor of the week. I wanted something more but I knew that it couldn't happen, and I worked for him now. Finally, around ten o'clock, I forced myself to stop thinking of him and go to sleep. Unfortunately, that was impossible and I went to sleep with his face imprinted in my head.

***

Ashton

After dropping Layla off at home, I drove home with a small smile on my face and her in my thoughts. Ever since I met her, I couldn't escape her. Everywhere I went and everything I did, I saw her in my head. After parking my 911 Carrera Porsche in my garage, I walked inside.

"Dude, why are you smiling?" a familiar voice asked as I passed by my living room. I stopped and turned to see Nick sitting on my couch.

"Why aren't you at your house?" I shot at him, but my tone wasn't as rude as I wanted it to be.

"You know I love your couch." He got up. I just rolled my eyes at him. Having known Nick since we were teens, I was used to him and his weirdness. "What's got you smiling?"

"Well…it's my new PA. It's the girl from the bar the other night," I told him, loosening my tie.

"The one with the cute dark-haired girl I danced with?"

"Yeah, her friend. Her name is Layla. I hired her to be my new assistant."

"So, she's the one occupying your time lately and who was in your thoughts at lunch today." I nodded. At lunch, my thoughts were stuck on her and I couldn't seem to concentrate on anything and ended our meeting early, wanting to get back to the office.

"Man, she has you wrapped around her finger, doesn't she?" Nick said, smirking at me. "Never would have thought I'd see the day Ashton Miller was hooked on a girl."

"Wait, I am not wrapped around her finger. Ashton Miller doesn't get hooked on a girl either. They get hooked on me."

"Then why are you smiling and thinking about her twenty-four seven?" I glared at him. I was not that guy who lusts after women; it was the opposite. Something about what he said though stuck in my head. Maybe I was getting hooked on her. That thought alone was worse than anything I could think of. No way was I going to let that happen to me; not again. From now on, I needed to stay away from Layla. I would not let my business and reputation get ruined over some girl. With that thought, I made it my goal to ignore Layla and go back to the way things were before I met her. Ever since I met her, things changed and they needed to get back to normal.

"Get out of my apartment," I growled at Nick and went back the way I came. I was going to get Layla out of my head.

***

I woke up the next morning to a hand running across my chest. I opened my eyes and stared at a pretty blonde stroking my head. I briefly remembered meeting her last night at a bar but wasn't too sure. I think her name was Emily.

"Good morning." The girl purred as she saw I was awake. I glanced around and was relieved to see we were in one of my guest bedrooms. I didn't ever sleep with someone in my own bed. We either go to one of my guest bedrooms, her apartment, or even do it at the bar in the bathroom. Seeing the sun was up and shining through the blinds, I knew I was late for work. I got up and started walking out the bedroom door ignoring the girl protesting behind me.

"Wait? Where are you going?" she asked as she trailed behind me only covered in a sheet. I turned around and looked at her. It didn't bother me that I stood naked in front of her. I could see her breasts through the sheet and almost wanted to take her back to the guest bedroom, but I stopped myself.

"Make sure you don't take anything on your way out. You know where the door is," I said and with that, I walked away from her. I felt her eyes on my back as I left her standing there but I ignored that. I was not going to lie but when I woke up, for a split second I though Layla was the one next to me. I guess going out and hooking up with a random girl, I still couldn't get my mind off of her.

I went to a bar last night hoping I couldn't find someone to get my mind off of her, but the entire night I kept comparing women to Layla. The more I did it, the more I got mad and soon I had lost count of how many drinks I had and I only remember grabbing some girl and taking her back here. I heard my front door slam shut as I walked through my bedroom door. I just shrugged as I made my way to my shower. I couldn't care less if that girl was pissed at me. It wasn't like I asked her to my girlfriend. Plus, I didn't plan on seeing her ever again. She should be happy right now; I gave her the best sex she will probably ever have.

I washed my body thoroughly in the shower, getting the smell of sex off of me, before stepping out. I saw on the clock that it was eight. Seeing as I was already late and that I was the boss, I took my time getting dressed. After putting on a gray suit, I went downstairs grabbing my keys and phone that I had thankfully remembered to put by the door last night. As I locked the door behind me and made my way to my car, I thought about last night. I could feel myself getting mad that I cheated on Layla, but I stopped it before it could get worse. *I didn't cheat on her. We aren't even together.* That thought did little to make me feel better.

As I drove to the office, I was shocked at what I was feeling. I was Ashton Miller. I didn't get feelings over a girl, and I sure as hell didn't feel bad about "cheating" on them. I had to start keeping my distance from Layla. She was making me feel things that I shouldn't. It would be hard since she now worked for me but I had to do it. With a plan inside my head, I got out of my car. I had to keep away from her and break whatever it was we have before it was too late, even if that meant I had to hurt to do so.

***

Layla

When I got to work the next morning, I was surprised to see Ashton wasn't already there. I even asked Judy where he was but she didn't know either. Sending him a quick text from my work phone, I headed to my office to start on my work. I had been up late into the night researching and studying up on everything I could about the company. If someone came up and asked me who were our biggest competitors, and who were our biggest beneficiaries I could tell you. I was really impressed with myself honestly. Who could have learned all that in just a few long hours?

I spent the next few hours setting up meetings for Ashton, talking to supervisors, and finishing the filing cabinet. Walking out of my office, I stared down at my phone making sure I hadn't missed a call or text from Ashton. I was starting to worry about him since I hadn't heard from him since last night. Sighing, I closed my phone and headed to the elevator. I had paperwork I needed to be signed and looked over by marketing. I wasn't entirely sure where to go, but I figured it couldn't be that hard to find. As I silently rode the elevator down, I remembered Neena said marketing was on either the twenty-fifth floor. Seeing that the elevator was stopping on that floor, I got out along with a few other people. I figured since I had to get these papers signed by the supervisor, I should head to the back where that person would have their office. Hopefully the floor was the same layout as mine or I was going to head in the wrong direction. After almost getting lost twice, I came to a stop in front of what looked to be a receptionist.

"Uh, hi," I said awkwardly to the lady. She looked to be in her mid-thirties and had a cute shoulder like cut to her hair. When she looked up at me, a pair of deep green eyes stared back at me.

"Hello. What can I do you for?" she asked politely.

"I'm here for Mrs. Johnson. I have some papers that need her approval and signature."

"She just met with someone but I can give them to you for her if you would like." I knew it was bad, but I felt relieved that she was gone. I wanted to get back upstairs and see if Ashton had come in yet, and I didn't want to talk to the lady forever as well. I knew I was being rude but I just didn't have it in me today.

"Yes, thank you so much. Just tell her that they don't need to be handed back until Friday. And when she is finished have her call my number," I said, sending the lady a smile. I didn't know if Mrs. Johnson would have my number, so I made sure to add it onto the papers with a sticky note. Thanking the lady once again, I headed back upstairs.

I said hi to a few people as I made my way back to Ashton's office and I was relieved to see Ashton standing next to Judy's desk. I picked up my pace, hard to do in my heels, and quickly came to a stop beside him.

"Ash—Mr. Miller, you are here," I said, fixing myself. I tried not to check him out which was very hard to do. He was wearing a nice gray suit that somehow made his bright blue eyes pop even more. His brown hair was styled in his sexy curly but slicked-back way. I could feel my stomach erupt into butterflies just looking at him. *Stupid feelings!*

"Ms. Kingston." He kept his eyes away from my face. "What did I miss?"

"Nothing. I just got back from giving those papers you asked me to give to Mrs. Johnson in marketing. I confirmed your twelve o'clock meeting with Mr. Holland. And I have a few things for you to look over before I can type up those reports to send to London; I sat them down on your desk earlier." I rattled off the things I had done and needed to do. I stood there feeling proud for it only come crashing down.

"I need you to go pick up my dry cleaning, make sure my maid has come to my house and cleaned up and that she had stocked the fridge up, and I need you to book me a reservation at Servantino's tomorrow night at seven," Ashton said to me. He was back to being cold when talking to me. I swallowed what I wanted to say to him when I remembered what Kacey had said. This was business Ashton; he would treat me like every other employee.

"I, uh, what?" I stuttered out, confused. He wanted me to run errands for him?

"Did I stutter?" He finally turned to me and glared at me, his voice as hard as a rock. I took a small step back from him. Seeing him glaring at me made me scared.

"I, uh, I n-no." I shook my head, my eyes wide.

"Good. I want it done and I expect you to be here at noon for my meeting to take notes. I need everything set up in the conference room, and that includes all the inquires of Mr. Holland's account, everything that has been used with his money, and a reason as to why he should stay with us." I stood there staring at him, confused. He had never talked to me this way before. From the corner of my eye, I even saw Judy staring at him wide-eyed.

"Sir, that's only two hours away from now!" It was a little after ten and he expected me to get that all done in two hours and still be at that meeting?

"Is that a problem? You are my PA, not some other employee. I expect one hundred and ten percent on this job. Just because I knew you before I hired you does not mean I will give you special treatment." He hissed at me. "If you cannot follow my orders, then I expect you to be put out on the street. I do not care that it is two hours away from now. I want it done and it will be done. If you cannot do that, then don't bother coming back at all." He leered down at me. With one last venom look, he stalked into his office.

I stared after him, feeling tears pooling in my eyes. Never had I seen someone look at me with such venom besides my father. I bit the inside of my cheek hard, tasting blood. Taking in a shaky breath and swallowing my tears, I headed to do what I was told. I was going to do everything Ashton told me to do in time and then shove it in his face.

Chapter 17

Layla

For the next two hours, I went all over hell and breakfast. Thankfully Ashton wasn't that rude to make me take a cab. Clark, Ashton's driver, was parked on the curb and seemed to be waiting for me. I didn't know if Ashton told him I was coming or Judy, but for some reason I thought Judy did it.

"Hello Clark," I said once I reached him.

"Hello, Ms. Kingston." Clark nodded at me and opened the door.

"Thank you." I slipped inside. A second later, Clark slid into the driver's seat.

"Where to?" he asked.

"Um, I don't know the address but Mr. Miller's dry-cleaning place?" I said. I was going to refer Ashton as Mr. Miller now after the way he talked to me.

"I know the place." He nodded and started driving in the right direction. While Clark drove to the dry cleaners, I decided I should make Ashton's dinner reservations. As I searched the number for the restaurant, I couldn't help but wonder why he needed a reservation and who he was going with. Even after he yelled at me and was completely rude, I couldn't stop the small feeling of hope that bloomed in my chest thinking that maybe he would be taking me.

I made the reservation under his name at seven, and by time I was done we were pulling up in front of the dry cleaners. Before Clark could open my door, I got out and told him I would be just a minute. I walked into the place and was struck with awe. This wasn't a typical dry cleaner. All different kinds of suits hung on mannequins all over the store, and it looked to also be a place where you buy suits instead of taking to get them clean. From where I stood at the door, I could see expensive named brands on the suits.

"Hello, how can I help you, miss?" an older man asked, coming up to me.

"Oh hi. I am here to pick up Mr. Miller's suits," I told the man.

"Right. This way." He turned and walked toward the back of the store. I followed behind him in awe at how many suits there were. The man went around the counter and went through a door I figured held all the suits. A minute later, he stepped back out with a big black bag. From the hangers sticking out of the top, I saw there were about six suits or so. "Here you go." He handed it to me. I grabbed it and tried not to show how heavy it was. Who knew suits were heavy!

"How much is it?" I asked.

"It's been taken care of. Let Mr. Miller we thank him." With that, the man walked out from behind the counter and walked over. *Okay.*

I awkwardly carried the six suits in my arms and to the car. Thankfully, Clark opened the door for me. I slid them in first along the seat, and then scooted in after. As I shifted the bag around, I told Clark to take me to Ashton's house. Two things down, three more to go. I checked my phone for the time and saw it was a quarter to eleven. I may just make it in time.

As we drove toward Ashton's house, I called Mr. Holland to confirm he would be there at noon. I got off the phone with his assistant just as we pulled up. I quickly got out and headed to the elevator to his floor. The annoying elevator music drifted around me as I rode up silently to Ashton's floor. A minute later, I came to a stop in front of his door and I realized I had no way to get inside. I quickly got out my phone and called Judy. It rang three times before she answered.

"Hello?"

"Hi Judy, it's Layla. I am at Ashton's house and I can't get in. Is there a code or a key?" I asked.

"On the right side of the wall is a key pad. Enter the code 1990, then when you leave, enter it again to lock the door."

"Thank you so much."

"You're welcome, honey." With that, she hung up.

I saw the keypad and entered the code. *How had I not noticed that before?* The keypad was high tech and asked if I wanted to unlock or lock the door.

Hitting unlock, I heard the door unlocking itself and the pad dinged to let me know it was open. I opened the door and trudged inside with the suits. I figured I should put them in his closet, so I walked up the stairs and into his room. Being back in the room reminded me of when I slept in the same bed as Ashton. I wasn't going to lie, that was the best I'd slept in a while. Pushing that thought away, I put the suits in a space in Ashton's closet.

Not wanting to be here any longer than necessary, I quickly shut the closet doors and went back downstairs remembering I was supposed to check if his maid cleaned up and stocked the fridge. My heels clicked on the tile floor as I walked to the kitchen. After seeing everything stocked up, I looked in the living room and saw everything was how it should look. Deciding everything was done there I walked out the door, pressed the code in, and made my way downstairs. It seemed I would make it back in time.

The whole way back I was glad I got in early today and already had most of the stuff for the meeting done. All I needed to do was get all of the stuff from Mr. Holland's account. We pulled up in front the company building at 11:30. I shouted a quick thank you to Clark before I was out of the car and running through the front doors. Neena sat at the front counter and I shot her a quick wave and smile before impatiently hitting the up button and tapping my heel against the ground.

I tried not to yell in frustration as the elevator took its time coming to a stop at the lobby. I had thirty minutes to get everything ready and taken to the conference room. Fortunately, the doors opened with a ding a few minutes later. I got pulled in along with about twenty other people. I was once again surrounded by the awkward elevator music. There was nothing worse than being packed inside an elevator with twenty or so other people and having to deal with the awkward silence. I had to stop myself from tapping my foot as we had to come to a stop at almost every floor.

By the time the doors opened to my floor I was fidgeting, anxious to hurry and show Ashton up. I knew who I had to go to, so instead of heading to my office I walked in the opposite direction, which I hoped was Liam's office. Seeing his name on a door up ahead, I quickened my pace. I knocked on the wooden door and waited to hear Liam telling me to go in. A faint "come in" reached my ears and I opened the door.

"Liam?" I asked, stepping into the room. His office was the complete opposite of Ashton's. Where Ashton had dark wood and couches, Liam had a tannish brown couch in the corner and a light brown desk. His walls were painted a pretty deep green color and he had a pretty view out the windows behind him; not as great as Ashton's, but still great.

"Layla! What are you doing here? Not that I don't mind that you are," he said, getting up out of his chair.

"Hi. Sorry for just coming by, but I need something from you." I came to a stop in front of his desk. I took a seat in one of the chairs in front of his desk. I noticed it wasn't as comfortable as

Ashton's. *Layla, stop!*

"Sure, what do you need?" He slipped back into his chair and turned to me.

"I need everything from Mr. Holland's account. I know it's so sudden but I need it like right now. I have a meeting with him in twenty minutes."

"Wow, cutting it short, aren't you?" he teased but noticed the look on my face and quickly turned to his computer. "It's no problem getting it. Just let me type his name in and print it off."

"Thank you, Liam, really," I said, relieved he could do it and hoping it took only just a second.

"No problem." We were quiet and the only sound that could be heard in the office was the sound of the computer keyboard and the mouse. Just a few minutes later, he turned to me. "There you go. They are just printing. I don't have a printer so it's down the hall." Before he even had the words out of his mouth, I was up and out of my seat.

"Thank you so much. I owe you!" I called over my shoulder as I left his office. I walked briskly to the copier room. By the time I made it there, most of the papers were printed off and I couldn't be more grateful. I made two other copies of them and stapled them together. I glanced at the clock on the wall and almost choked. I had less than three minutes to get to the conference room before Ashton and Mr. Holland.

If someone would have seen me right now they would have thought I had ran a marathon or something. My hands were shaking and my face felt flushed as I opened the conference door and practically threw the papers on the table. I felt like I had drunk five cups of coffee. I sat my bag I still had on my shoulder on a chair, and straightened out the papers. As soon as I smoothed out my skirt, the door opened and in walked Ashton and who I assumed was Mr. Holland.

I turned and plastered a smile on my face as they turned to me. I would have liked to see surprise or even admiration on Ashton's face when he saw I was there on time, but there were no emotions on his face. His face was blank and his blue eyes stared down at me as he walked to his chair at the head of the table.

"And who is this?" Mr. Holland asked Ashton as he walked around the table to his seat. He looked to be in his late fifties and had some gray in his brown hair at the temples. Wrinkles circled his brown eyes and mouth. He looked like a man who has laughed a lot, but at the same time can be serious when he needs to. I opened my mouth to answer but Ashton beat me to it.

"No one of importance. So, Henry, I brought you here so you can see exactly what has been happening with your money and our company," Ashton said. I bit back the hurt at how he just brushed me off to the side and took a seat to the right of him and across from Mr. Holland. My mind started to wander as Ashton talked to Mr. Holland about his stuff. I was starting to feel the ache in my feet and my head was starting to hurt. I was hoping this meeting wouldn't be too long so I could go eat.

"Ms. Kingston." The sound of my name being called jerked me out of my thoughts. I blinked, clearing my eyes and saw both men staring at me.

"Yes?" I asked, hoping I wouldn't get in trouble for not paying attention.

"Henry here wants to know what you think about his investments," Ashton said, his jaw clenched. He stared at me angry, almost like it was my fault Mr. Holland wanted my opinion.

"You want my opinion, sir?" I asked, making sure they were asking the right thing. Mr. Holland nodded at me. I sat up straighter in my chair.

"Well, sir, in my opinion I wouldn't go anywhere else but here. Nowhere else will you get a full review of all your investments and the truth of what your money is going to. You are trusting us to put your money to good use and to make you more money in return, right? Yes, you could go somewhere else and maybe get the same result but other companies weren't built the way this one is. It is family based and everyone here has the same goal: to make sure the money we are entrusted with goes to a good cause. The best part about Miller Industries is you can go online right now and search up about anything you want about us. You can see our numbers, data, what our money goes to. What other companies would do that? I am not going to try too hard to convince you that we are the right choice. It is your money and you have the full decision to what you want with it," I said.

He sat there staring at me for a full minute before he opened his mouth.

"I like this girl. Is she your PA?" Mr. Holland asked, turning to Ashton. Ashton stared at me before looking at Mr. Holland and nodded. "It's nice seeing someone knowing what the business does in depth. Mr. Miller, you don't have to worry about me leaving. I know I am in good hands. I better get going I have to go have lunch with my wife." He stood up and shook Ashton's hand. He nodded at me and left the room. I watched him leave and then turned to Ashton. He sat there stiffly clenching his jaw and I thought I saw his fists being clenched underneath the table.

"Ashton, you okay?" I asked softly. I felt like I needed to approach Ashton slowly, almost like he was a caged animal.

"No, I am not," he said, his voice so hard it could cut rocks. I sat still in my chair staring at him. "I was going to wait until later to do this but I am not going to." I felt something drop in my stomach and I knew something bad was about to happen. *Am I going to get fired? I did everything he has asked of me. It's only been two days. How much damage could I have done?* Questions flew into my mind as I waited for Ashton to talk.

"We are done. Whatever we had is over and was never real. I do not want to keep going on and pretending anymore. I never liked you. I only went out with you out of pity and because I felt the need to after saving you from those guys in that alley. I mean hell, look at you. Who would like you? It's no wonder you are single. You're nothing worth bragging about. Someone like me doesn't belong to someone like you; you're too low class for me and honestly not worth it."

Every word that came out of his mouth was like a stab to the stomach. I stared at him wide-eyed, not wanting to believe what he was saying. He looked at me with a cold, blank expression. "I shouldn't have gone on as long as I did, but who doesn't like a good chase now and again?" He shrugged like it was nothing. "I will let you keep your job since it seems you need it by the look of your apartment. I still expect your work to be unaffected and done correctly. Now, if you will excuse me, I have someone I have to go have lunch with." With that last word, he got up and walked out of the conference room leaving me sitting there stunned and with my eyes stinging.

I didn't know what to say or even think. My eyes burned as unshed tears started to fill them. *Not worth it. Never liked you. Low class. Never real.* I shook my head at myself feeling stupid for even thinking Ashton could at all like me. Stupid, pathetic girl. Of course, it wasn't real. I should have known someone like him wouldn't go for someone like me. A traitorous tear escaped my eye and trailed down my cheek. I wiped it away. I stood up on shaky legs and took a deep, shuddering breath. I didn't think I can stay the rest of the day, especially like this. Trying to compose myself, I grabbed my bag and left the room heading to Judy's desk.

"Judy," I croaked out then coughed to clear my throat. She looked up at me and her face instantly morphed into concern.

"Layla, are you okay?"

"I, uh, no. Is it okay if I take the rest of the day off? Mr. Miller knows," I lied. "I know it's a lot to ask but I don't feel well."

"Of course, dear. I will take care of everything. If you can't make it in tomorrow as well, just let me know," Judy said, smiling sadly at me. I nodded in thanks, grateful she didn't press for details.

With my head down, I quickly walked to the elevator and out the front doors. I jumped into a random cab, barely remembering to tell the man my address. Once the cab started driving, I let my tears come. I stared out the window and saw my reflection staring back at me. Tears escaped my gray eyes that were starting to turn back to their regular lifelessness. My bottom lip trembled as I tried not to sob out loud. As I stared at my face, I felt anger toward myself bubbling up inside of me. *Stupid fucking face. You aren't worth anything!* No sooner than I thought that, the cab came to a stop at my building and I handed the man some cash not bothering to say anything as I got out and slammed the door. I knew Kacey wouldn't be there as I made my way up the stairs. This morning she told me she had some fashion show thingy to go to. I opened my door and let my bag drop. As soon as my bag hit the floor, heart-wrenching sobs burst free. It was those silent sobs that made your whole body ache and no sound to come out of your lungs. I collapsed on my bed and sobbed as I replayed Ashton's words to me over and over.

***

Ashton

I left the conference room fighting not to turn back and run to Layla and tell her everything I said was a lie. I knew I hurt her, maybe too much, but it was for her own good. She would be thanking me one day that I ended it before it even began. She had to know that I didn't have a heart and what I was capable of. Hurting women was what I did and Layla needed to realize that.

Walking past Judy and her questioning eyes, I left the building and slid into my car. Clark pulled away from the curb and drove me to where I was meeting Natasha for lunch. I took a deep breath and stared at the window, trying my hardest not to feel bad for breaking Layla's heart.

Chapter 18

Layla

I spent the whole night holed up in my room not bothering to leave to eat, shower, or even to talk to Kacey. Part of me knew I was over exaggerating since I had only known Ashton for a week, but another part of me was really hurt at his words. I had heard the words plenty of times to know they were true, but having them come from someone you didn't think would say them to you hurt worse than anything; worse than when my parents told me the same things.

Dinner had passed a while ago and I lay in bed staring at nothing, and hearing my stomach growl loudly through the room. My stomach was begging me to eat, but I didn't want to get up. As I stared at nothing, my door flew open and in walked Kacey glaring at me.

"Layla Ann Kingston, you are getting out of that bed this instant," she said, her voice low and dangerous. I rolled my head to the side and stared at her. I knew my face was not at all attractive at the moment. I bet I had mascara running down my cheeks, my eyes swollen and cheeks blotchy. I wish I was one of those girls who could look great while crying, but sadly I was stuck with looking like a zombie when I cried. If she was scared of my face, she didn't show it. When I didn't make any movement, she marched over to my bed and threw my duvet away from me.

"You are going to get up. Shower to get your clown-looking face off, and then you are going to eat. While you are eating, you are going to tell me everything." She grabbed my arm in a hard grip and pulled me straight off the bed. I squeaked in surprise at her strength. For someone so small, she sure was strong. "Get your ass in the shower right now while I grab you something to eat." With that demand, she shoved me toward my bathroom and left the room. I sighed and headed to the bathroom.

Stripping out of my wrinkled work clothes, I stepped into the warm shower and let the warmth surround me. I thoroughly washed my hair and body, trying to get the day off of me. I stood in the water until it turned cold, then I finally got out. Wrapping a towel around me, I left the bathroom not even bothering to look in the mirror. I knew what I looked like and I didn't want to scare myself. I pulled on my fluffiest pair of PJ bottoms and an old oversized shirt my last boyfriend left with me. Quickly running the towel through my hair, I brushed it and left my room, letting my hair air dry.

Slumping down on the couch, I stared at the TV. Not even a second later, Kacey put a bowl down on my lap and I saw she made me ramen noodles in soup form. Otherwise known as cheap college food. I shot her a grateful smile and started to eat. I didn't know I was that hungry as I gobbled down my soup.

"Now that you are cleaned up and eating, care to explain to me why I came home to find you sobbing on your bed when you should be at work?" Kacey said, cutting the silence. I swallowed and looked down trying to gather my thoughts and say it without making Kacey lose her shit. "Wait! Was it your parents? Are they here?"

My head snapped up and I quickly shook it. If my parents were here, then the world would be ending. Kacey's shoulders relaxed as she stared at me.

"I...Ashton broke up with me," I finally spit out. I surprised myself with what I said. Ashton and I weren't really an item. Why did I say it like we were? We only went on one official date.

"At work?" she asked, anger laying underneath the surface.

"Yeah. I know we weren't really anything and I am overreacting," I said, twirling some noodles around my fork.

"He said something, didn't he! What did he say to make you look this horrible?" I shot her a glare. Only Kacey would be thinking about how bad I looked.

"It was nothing, Kay. I don't want to talk about it."

"Layla," she warned.

"No. Kacey, it was really nothing. Nothing I haven't heard before anyways. I don't know why I am acting this way. I knew what he was like and I should have known I couldn't change someone like him," I said.

Kacey just stared at me. I gave her a look that said drop it and I heard her sigh.

"Fine, I will drop it. But if I see him I won't hesitate to kick him in the balls, just saying." She shot me a grin. "He let you keep your job as his PA?"

"Yeah, he did. It's going to be hard seeing him every day but I am not going to quit and let him think I am weak," I said. "Plus, tomorrow is Thursday and then Friday so I won't have to see him for two days." I finished my soup and got up to put the dish in the dishwasher. Just as I walked out of the room, I heard Kacey shout and her footsteps coming in my direction.

"I know what you need to do," she said proudly. I looked at her and was afraid to ask what. When she got that look on her face, I knew what she was thinking wouldn't be good. I looked at her hesitantly before asking her what she had in mind. "You need to look hot while at work. Show him what he is missing out on." After she said it, she got a proud smile on her face like she had cured cancer or something.

"Kay, I can't dress provocatively at work. It's a multi-million-dollar company. I can't have my ladies showing!" I gestured to my chest. Kacey just rolled her eyes.

"Layla, I am not saying wear a hooker outfit. I am saying you need to wear tighter clothes to show off your hot body, and maybe a few inches shorter of skirts so your long legs can be seen." I instantly shook my head at her.

"No way in hell, Kacey! You know I am not like that! Just wearing one of your pencil skirts I felt like I was on display for everyone." I continued to argue with her but she didn't budge.

And that was how I ended up looking the way I did as I headed to work the next day. Kacey had gotten up way before me and came barging into my room shouting for me to wake up. Being the she-devil she was, she shoved me off the bed and ignored the dagger glares I sent her. Not even waiting for me to get up by myself, she gripped my upper arm and hauled me up and into her room. Shoving what looked to be a small piece of fabric into my hands, she almost stripped me out of my own clothes. When Kacey was like this, I couldn't help but feel scared. I knew if I didn't comply she would rip my head off and keep it as her trophy.

I grabbed what I realized was a dress and started slipping it on. I had to tug on the material and finally got it in the right place. Thankfully, the dress was kind of stretchable so it fit my frame but it clung to my body almost like a second skin. I felt like my boobs were up to my ears and that my butt was on display. I turned and looked in the mirror and had to admit the dress was really pretty. It was a dark gray color and had a small brown belt around the waist. The dress was just the right amount of professionalism.

"Man, Layla, if I was a dude I'd so do you," Kacey said behind me. I raised an eyebrow at her. "Anyways, let's get to work on your hair." With that, she pushed me onto her chair and got to work. About twenty minutes later I was staring at someone else in the mirror. My long brown hair was curled and hung down my back. My gray eyes popped as Kacey did a dark sultry look on my eyes. My cheeks were thankfully lightly caked with makeup, just enough to make it look natural. She handed me the same pair of heels I'd been wearing the past couple of days.

I slipped those on and stood up. As I stared in the mirror, I couldn't help but feel excited to see Ashton's face. Kacey made me look hot and I was surprisingly happy with the look. I was going to show Ashton he messed with the wrong girl, and that I was nothing like what he said I was. With a determined look, I hugged Kacey and thanked her before grabbing stuff and heading to the office.

Watch out, Ashton Miller, Layla Kingston is about to show you up.

***

I walked into work, shot Neena a hi, and walked to the elevator. The moment I stepped out onto my floor, I felt like everyone's eyes were on me. I kept my head up and ignored everyone as I walked to my office. I was not going to let Ashton know he had hurt me. If he wanted to play a game then I was going to play, but on my own terms. Saying hi to Judy, I went to my office and opened up my phone and computer to see what I had to do today. I didn't even bother to see if Ashton was here before I got to work.

Soon enough noon hit, and I hadn't seen Ashton all day. A little part of me was bummed that I didn't because I wanted to show off but the other part of me was glad. I didn't know how I was going to react seeing him. I headed downstairs to the small cafeteria the company had. I hadn't been down there yet and thought might as well check it out. Just as I stepped out of the elevator, Neena came into view. She was just leaving the front counter and seemed to be headed to where I think the cafeteria was located.

"Neena!" I called out and picked up my pace. Thankfully she heard me, as did almost everyone else. Ignoring all the weird looks I got from people, I came to a stop next to her. "Hey," I said with a smile.

"Wow, Layla, you look very hot today," she commented and wiggled her eyebrows at me. I couldn't help but laugh.

"Thank you. I love your outfit as well," I said noticing that she was wearing a dress like mine but less form-fitting and a little more professional. "I was wondering if I could eat with you today?"

"Of course! I could always use someone to sit with. Usually, I just sit by myself in the cafeteria."

"Well, from now on consider me your new lunch buddy," I said with a smile. She smiled back and we headed to get something to eat. Apparently, the cafeteria was at the back of the building and in a pretty big room. As we walked in, I saw the place had basically everything. It almost looked like a buffet. I followed Neena to one of the counters and saw salads, sandwiches, and even full plates of food with spaghetti.

"I like the salads here but basically everything is good. They sure know how to feed us right here," she joked as she grabbed a good-looking salad. I looked around and saw a place that had slices of pizza and immediately went over to it. I grabbed two slices of pepperoni and turned around. I spotted Neena over by a machine that looked like one of those where you put ice cream in it and it stirs it for you.

"What is this?" I asked.

"A coffee machine. Well, more like a Frappuccino machine. Pick whatever you want from here." She pointed to a big freezer on the side. "And put it in here and it blends it for you. It is honestly the best thing ever invented." Her drink was finished in a matter of seconds. I looked at all the kinds and my eyes landed on my favorite flavor. I quickly grabbed the hazelnut and put it in the machine. Clicking thick, I waited almost impatiently for it. I'd been a while since I had a Frappuccino, and my mouth was actually watering. Once it was finished, Neena led me to a table in the corner and sat down.

"You're having pizza?" she asked, surprised.

"Yeah." I shrugged and took a sip of my coffee. I almost moaned but stopped myself. Wow, was it good! I forced myself to set it down, instead of sucking the whole thing down in minutes. Grabbing one slice of my pizza, I bit into it. Okay, this place had amazing food!

"Good, huh?" She took a bite of her salad.

"Yes, it is. Wow. I wouldn't have thought the

cafeteria here would be this good."

"Well, being a multi-million-dollar company has its perks." I nodded and continued to stuff my face.

We spent the rest of our lunch hour talking and getting to know one another. Neena and I had a lot in common and I knew Kacey would like her too. I learned that her parents were both professors at NYU, *I actually had one of her parents as my History professor*, she had just graduated around the same time as me, that she had a younger brother who was in his second year at Yale University, and that she wanted to become a magazine editor or anything to do with stuff like that. She would definitely get along with Kacey just fine. I told her the basics of my life, not going into much detail. It was a little after one when we decided we better get back to work. After inviting her to do something this weekend, I headed back to my office.

The rest of the afternoon passed fairly quickly and I hadn't seen Ashton all day. As four o'clock passed, I figured he hadn't come in today and I couldn't help but sigh. A good outfit went to waste. I was finishing up a few last things before heading home when my work phone buzzed. Looking over at it, I saw Ashton's name on the screen.

To: Layla
From: Mr. Miller
Need you in my office ASAP.

That was all it said. I didn't let myself think that he wanted to apologize to me. I knew he wouldn't. He was not that kind of guy; others apologized, but not Ashton. Knowing I better not keep him waiting, I left my office and headed to his. I didn't even bother to knock and walked right in. Ashton sat at his desk writing something down and didn't even look up.

"You needed me, Mr. Miller?" I said, keeping my voice neutral.

"Yes. Anything important happen today while I was gone?" he asked, still keeping his head down. I stared him down and tried to make him look up at me.

"No, sir. Is that all you needed?" Just staring at him made his words come screaming back in my mind. I forced them down and kept my face blank. I was good at hiding being hurt. I'd been doing it since I was thirteen, so it wouldn't be a problem now.

"No, Ms. Kingston. Every year we host a benefit party and everyone who is anyone attends. Things are auctioned off, toasts are made, and business is discussed. This benefit will take place in two weeks. It is your job to get everything ready." Ashton sat up and finally looked at me. I saw his blue eyes widen as he stared at me but as soon as I blinked, they were back to normal. "That includes invitations, booking a venue, drinks delivered, things to be auctioned off, and to make sure it all runs smoothly. It should start about seven the latest." He stared at me almost like he was bored.

"In two weeks?" I sputtered out. How in god's name would I get everything done in two weeks!?

"Yes. It will be held on September twenty-fifth." Today was the tenth, so tomorrow it would be two weeks. I had to try very hard not to glare at his stupid face as he stared at me blankly. He was only doing this to get under my skin. Fine. If that's what he wanted, then he would get it. If he wanted to see if I would fail, he was going to be sadly mistaken.

"Okay, sir. I will get right on that. Anything else?" I barely controlled my anger. He seemed almost surprised when I didn't give him a reaction.

HA! Layla: 1 Ashton: 0.

"No, nothing else." I gave him a nod and turned to leave. "Oh yeah, did you make my reservation tonight?" he called before I made it through the door and out to safety.

"Yes, I did. Serventino's at seven." I shut the door behind me.

Well, your plan didn't work, Kacey. I headed back to my office. Ashton didn't even spare me a second glance. I was starting to wonder if I even did see that flicker of something in his eyes. I shook my head at myself, feeling pathetic at how I wanted Ashton to react to my slutty outfit.

Not having anything else to do today, I grabbed my stuff and left the office. I hailed a taxi and headed home. *Well, Layla, today didn't turn out as planned. Ashton didn't even notice the way you dressed today, and you got even more work to do even though you just started two days ago.* I sighed and stared at the buildings as we passed them. If this was how things were going to be from now on, I wasn't so sure I wanted to keep doing it.

Coming Soon

MY PERFECT SALVATION

Perfect Series, Book Two

By: Kenadee Bryant

Acknowledgements

I want to say thank you to my mom for encouraging me to send this book in. She has always been by my side and has helped me in every way possible. Thank you to everyone on Wattpad for supporting me and my writing. For reading this book when I first started it three years ago and sticking with me through it all. Without you I wouldn't be here today.

Huge thank you to everyone at Limitless for helping me with this book and the whole process. Without my amazing editor and the others this book would still be locked in my computer.

About the Author

Currently lives in a small town called Mesquite, Nevada. She is going to college to be an English teacher and writes on the side. When she isn't busy with school work or writing new books she likes to hang out with her family, do things outdoors, and read whatever she can get her hands on.

Facebook:
https://www.facebook.com/kenadee.bryant

Twitter:
https://twitter.com/kendoll350

Goodreads:
https://www.wattpad.com/user/OutOfMyLimit17